STEP INTO THE DREAM

Finding love and realising dreams.

Note on Names and Places:

The names of characters, places, and events depicted in this work are fictitious. Any resemblance to actual persons, living or dead, or to actual events or locales is purely coincidental.

This disclaimer is intended to protect the author from any potential legal claims or misunderstandings that may arise from the reader's interpretation of the fictional elements in the work. It is important to note that while the characters, places, and events may be fictional, the author may have drawn inspiration from real-world experiences or knowledge. However, any similarities to real-world entities are unintentional and should not be taken as fact.

By reading this work, the reader acknowledges that the content is purely fictional and that any reliance on the information contained within is at their own risk. The author is not responsible for any consequences that may result from the reader's interpretation or use of the information presented in the novella.

PREFACE

In the grand tapestry of life, we are often faced with choices that shape our destinies. Society, family, and societal expectations can weave intricate patterns, guiding us towards paths that might not align with our hearts. For some, these paths lead to fulfilling lives, while for others, they can feel confining and stifling.

This book is a testament to the courage it takes to break free from these pre-determined paths and embark on a journey towards self-discovery and fulfilment. It is a tale of an individual who dared to question societal norms, defied parental expectations, and pursued his dreams with unwavering determination.

Through his stories, we will explore the challenges and triumphs of following one's heart, the complexities of family dynamics, and the transformative power of love. We will discover that even when faced with adversity, it is possible to find joy, purpose, and meaningful connections.

This book is dedicated to those who have ever felt trapped by societal expectations, those who have yearned for a different path, and those who have found the courage to pursue their dreams, no matter the obstacles. May it inspire you to embrace your authentic self, to follow your heart, and to create a life that truly resonates with your soul.

Scene 01

"Home is where the heart is, but it can also be where the chaos is." – Unknown

His heart was heavier to carry, too shattered for my mundane eyes to look at, his smile so encrypted you could almost believe it. From my blurry standpoint, I could clearly see as his lips moved in silence to say, "Unfortunately you don't get to choose your parents" and even clearer as his frown transitioned to an almost perfect smile for the guests.

At this point, I felt like a tiny God, and I admired it, taking the front seat and perfect googles to gape at as Matthew crumbly put one foot in front of the other. However, like all paths even his had smooth sails giving my jaws small breaks and my cheeks good exercises as I plunge into smiles and envy. Fortunately, his was not a story of love and that kept my tears intact, see am not a hater of the L word, I have just had my heart shattered a few times and I stopped believing, not in love rather in human's ability to nurture it.

Okay, before I spill the beans about myself, let me hop onto my Godly seat and buckle up. Matthew Nkosi is an 18-year-old young man who is lucky to have his whole life planned out, only he has done no planning. His parents Mr and Mrs Nkosi who are both aspiring politician and lawyer took the liberty to ensure they engrave his path for him. He spent every bit of his free time glued to a computer screen with the intent on of becoming a computer genius and guru. With his super brain Matthew managed to impress his not so easy to impress parents right from kindergarten up to his high school senior year with straight A's and top of his class, adding as a bonus his acceptance to the California Institute of Technology.

Matthew was born and bred in the rural areas of Western cape, surrounded by smooth hills, beautiful rocks, cocky hens, and friendly goats in a small township called Ebenezer. Owed to the success of his parents he was groomed in a fancy hill mansion, went to the best schools, and never lacked for anything his whole life. He had the best technologies coupled with his urge of curiosity to pursue his parents dream and help him fall in love with computers. Matthew grew up a computer nerd, only he was not.

"Yes, right at the T-junction take a left headed up the hill, you will not miss it" and she yelled Hunny! Hunny! How do I look? Before Mr Nkosi could answer she continued to say, "hurry up that was the judge and his wife on the phone we should welcome them together."

It was an evening of the 31st of December 2023, the summer breeze still intact, sun half gone and the road to the Nkosi family was filled with luxurious cars, from Porsche to Mercedes. lawyers, judges, politicians, and every bit of influential people were all headed up to the Nkosi mansion to see the Nkosi trophy. Even I cannot resist the spirit of celebrating a year end and stepping into another one looking forward to better opportunities and growth, but I can admit, the Nkosis were celebrating in style.

Amidst the celebrations, the inspiration and the Influence that had filled the Nkosi mansion that evening, to Matthew it was all chaos, and he has never felt so lonely in such a huge crowd. All that he was looking forward to was the arrival of his lady friend Elsa. Everything made sense whenever she was around. He kept pacing around his room and looking at his phone waiting to hear from her that she has arrived. Finally, after pacing for what seemed like a good 20km, he received a text that reads "I just got done freshening up, I will be there in no time bae." This was not the smile I saw earlier, this was his genuine smile, and it was a better sight to watch.

As Mrs Nkosi was busy with her ups and downs, there she was taking a few steps back thinking she had seen someone she recognized, to her surprise it was indeed someone she recognized, Elsa was crawling up the mansion shyly, her eyes were fixated to the luxurious cars parked outside. Before she knew it as she was taking out her phone from the purse to text Matthew of her arrival, Mrs Nkosi was on her face, I can swear if one would say she moved with the speed of light towards Elsa I would not dispute.

Everything she did that day seemed to be of haste, but this was not just haste, a real sense of urgency was vividly displayed just in those two seconds she moved towards Elsa. Well, let me who saw it all tell you a bit about it. She was nicely parading her mansion right before she spotted Elsa, right then and there she grabbed her dress from the bottom with her right hand, I don't remember her heels touching the ground, she flew straight to Elsa.

Luckily, I am gifted at reading people and emotions, otherwise I would have been seeing what everyone else was seeing, if I did not know better, I would say Mrs Nkosi was exhilarated to see Elsa, which I could clearly see she was not. But then again, I am no expert I could be wrong, before Elsa could even unlock her phone, she gently held her hand and whispered to her face what only she heard, and God knows.

The Nkosis sure know how to throw a party and hold it down, the food was amazing, the music was top notch, and champagne glasses flew around the room, except Matthew kept to himself cooped up in his room still pacing and trying to get hold of Elsa with no luck. "Boy! Boy! you know this party is to celebrate you right? we are so proud of you for all you have achieved and finally your dream is about to come true, and you are still this shy?" Mrs nkosi said jokingly while fixing Matthew's tie and collars.

She left his room with a smile on her face, and she told him to come out and enjoy his party. The party was a blast, and the programme went on and on until came a time when the hosts had to say a few words and Mrs Nkosi did not want to present the Nkosi trophy without its vicinity, right before she could climb the stage, she went rushing to Matthew's room.

"Matthew! what is wrong with you?" she said rashly and harshly as she enters his room without even a single knock, I guess her high heels did the knocking as you could hear them amidst the music and the noises, that is how fast and boldly she stormed into his room. You should see me well seated with my head rolling up, down and to the sides trying to get a perfect view, I live for the disputes, don't I? well without further ado she grabbed him by his hand helping him stand up and she gave him the shout of his life. She made sure he knew the party was to celebrate him and how proud she is of him adding with that he should not embarrass her, all in one shout. Her words were brief, and he straight up followed her to the stage, He encrypted an almost perfect smile for the guests.

Scene 02

"The next best thing to the enjoyment of a good time is the recollection of it"-James Lendall Basford

"Hunny would you please stop pacing and relax, he probably just went to say his goodbyes to his friends" said Mr Nkosi to an extremely anxious Mrs Nkosi. For a moment there I wished I could just go in and taser her to a deep sleep, no! not cruel that pacing was really starting to give me a terrible headache. She slowly sat on the bed next to where he was laying and asked, "papa which friends could he have possibly gone to? you know your son does not have any actual friends right?"

As she worry, and with Mr Nkosi trying to put out the fire in her worries, Matthew was well intact and safe. He did not have a single scratch on his body, except he had a lot more wounds on his brains. His sense of fulfilment was losing light with every breath he took.

Walking in nature can be soothing, I saw it working for Matthew. Walking barefoot helps to improve the sensory feedback as there are several nerve endings on the feet which are exposed directly to the stimuli, except Matthew was not that well informed as he stepped out of the Toyota Corolla, he had the privilege of driving as his own, he stepped out barefooted. I have never seen a person so eager for a peace of mind like he was, he climbed up the Zwart Berg mountain as if there was a door to a different universe full of peace. Well, we are not here to judge and criticize the boy, are we?

He ascended the mountain exhausted as a farm horse, with his blood boiling up and his heart racing for peace, his mind was yearning to be cleared. Before he could catch a breath, he took out his phone and dialled Elsa, it went straight to voice mail like every five minutes he tried to call her since the previous night when she failed to show up at the Nkosi's New Year's Eve party. Elsa was nowhere to be reached and that was just the tip of the iceberg to his burning heart and drowning mind.

There is never a better time for mountains to be this beautiful in South Africa except during the summer season, everything so green, the ground so rich and smooth, flowers blossoming, most plant at their healthiest, the breeze so perfect. I swear if I had a chance to capture and name this beauty, I wouldn't let my mind wonder trying to find non-existing words I was just going to say "heaven". By the way I will come back to this peace of heaven and tell you all about it, today we are here for our boy Matthew. Well, I must admit that I did really forget about him there for a moment, not intentionally though, but now I understand why he came to free his mind here gazing at all this beauty and a perfect view of the village.

There he was picking a wildflower and reminiscing about the first day he brought

Elsa to this spot and gave her the same flower, I am glad to say that the memory did put a smile on the young man's face. I remember that day like it was my first time believing in love, Matthew and Elsa had been crushing on each other since they started high school, and he finally got the courage to ask her out when they were doing grade ten (10). He took her up the hill holding her left hand, as sweaty as the hands were from climbing, they never let go. They continued taking short breaks and he would look her straight into the eyes with so much admiration, the boy would not stop giggling all the way through.

I do not know how they did it, but the only time Matthew would take a deep breath was when she would also look back into his eyes, not because of a racing heart from being tired, his heart raced full of love. They climbed the mountain as easy as a pie. As for Elsa it was as though her whole body became numb since he took her hand and held it. Before they could get to the top of the mountain, he took out a handkerchief from his pocket and gave it to her to wrap around her eyes. Elsa is a very strong-willed lady, and she refused to put it over her eyes.

He moved slowly around her to her back, as she turned her head to look back at him, he held her gently behind the ears and pointed her heard forward, he grabbed her from the waist, he slowly moved his palms around her pelvic girdles till they met by her abdomen. She closed her eyes for a moment and took the deepest breath, her whole body shivered. He leaned to her right ear and whispered, "do you trust me?" no words could come out her mouth, the only reaction she could give was shutting her eyes and her heart propelled her to signal yes, she nodded. He took the handkerchief from her hand and put it over her eyes and tied it from the back. There he was being all Superman, he carried her on his back towards the top of the Zwart berg.

For a moment I found myself drooling to the sight of these two love birds. When they got to the top, he gently put her down. As she was reaching for the handkerchief, he held both her hands and said "no! wait!" with a faint voice trying to catch a breath. Well truth be told he was tired and trying to hide it, I did say he was trying to be superman to impress the young lady by carrying her, I mean he is not even that muscular, what a silly boy. He took a moment to catch his breath, and he said to her "I am going to remove it now and this is the best sight you going to grasp at" it was getting darker and darker with each second that lapsed; he took off the handkerchief from her back and stood in silence, waiting for her reaction to the beauty of the village.

It was as though Matthew had a concurrence with the village, light started coming on in what seemed like a sequence, lighting up the whole village with different kind of lights, the moment was absolutely amazing. It even looked like God himself had said "LET THERE BE LIGHT". Elsa stood there with her mouth wide open, no words coming out. She turned to him; her eyes were flooded with tears. Everything she was looking at got blurry, she reached to hug him, she put her arms around his neck, her being shorter to him she was standing like a kangaroo tiptoed, he put his arms around her waist, and they squeezed tight.

There I was feeling sleepy wondering when they would let each go, it was dark for heaven's sake, especially for kids to be at this distance away from home. No! am not jealous rather concerned about their safety. Okay after a moment the hug eased up and she said, "thank you Matthew this is indeed beautiful, gorgeous even." Without saying a word, he took out the wildflower from his back pocket and gave it to her, as I was wondering when he picked that up, she took it, looked down on it and said "Maaa-tthew" with a huge smile and a shy voice. Her dimples have never been so beautiful.

From that day I told myself I need to get myself some young and exciting love, well I haven't yet, am not in a hurry anyway. Matthew looked into her eyes and said, "Elsa will you please be my girlfriend?" and there was a pause with dreading silence, she also looked up to him and said "I wish I could say yes, but at the moment, I am spoken for" the disappointment in his eyes was as vivid as the Christmas sun. His disappointment was followed by a kick to reality and his senses came back, he took out his phone to check the time. "Flip, my mother is going to kill me, let's go." He led the way, and she was behind him, before they could lose site of the vicinity of the village she hung back and called him "Matthew" when he turned back, she hugged him and said "thank you, this was sweet" before he could open his mouth with a remark, she kissed him.

Matthew laughed to the memory of the two kissing, and that moment gave life to his soul, his face brightened, and I was overjoyed that he came up here. He was finally in the realm of peace. He took out his phone again and entered his chats with Elsa cracking his head trying to find out what could have gone wrong. Wondering if he said something that would have offended her. He scrolled up, he scrolled down, up again, down again to his last text that reads "babe I understand you could have been shy to come, it is okay I survived the night, meet me at our favourite spot in the evening, I want to say my goodbyes, I miss you."

He looked up the sky and it was brighter and more beautiful than a day light, it was a fine night with an astounding bright half-moon, the sky was filled up with a bunch of stars. Well, he was actually looking up to God, but no one could resist that beautiful look, and if anyone were to look for a place where God would be, that was a beautiful night to believe it would be up the sky. He stepped back from the edge of the mountain, he took a sit on a rock. His eyes were watery, and he couldn't help it, as he sat on the rock tears started dripping off from his right eye, and the left one got blurrier by the heartbeat.

He looked up the sky trying to get his tears to fall back into where they came from, unfortunately for him, his efforts were in vain. He put his hands on the face, each palm over each eye slowly dragged them down with a heavy breath that birthed the words "oh God." I am quite certain right in that moment HE ripped open Matthew's heart and took a better look inside of it before he could even utter any words. "Who am I? why God why? all I want is for you to reveal to me my talents and desires, all my life I have known computers and nothing about them get me exhilarated, if only you could reveal to me the gift, I wrapped up my fists when I was born, I would be very glad" he took a sigh of relief like he had just confronted his scariest monster.

It is a worldly myth or rather a fact known to all, including those who do not believe in God that each person is born with their fists rolled up, not necessarily to fight, but protecting all the gifts they have, yet some live their whole lives without realizing them, while others make a fortune out of them. How is that? Could it be possible that some are protecting nothing and only the chosen ones come with gifts? If so, what kind of algorithm is used? These were some amongst the many more questions that were roaming in Matthew's head. Matthew was tired of living his parent's dream and excelling in what he did not like and enjoy, only at that moment he never knew anything else he can do better. He never knew love; all he knew was the imprisonment of his parent's praises and encouragements to study computer science.

"We are all born with a genius. But the problem is that most people never find it"- Albert Eistein

"Do not get me wrong lord I am grateful for all that I have, having grown not wanting for anything, I am grateful for all the fortunes, but I do not want to serve my parent's purpose I want to find my own purpose" he said with a guilty voice and his whole face was up in shame and full of guilt. Finally, he was able to get rid of all the tears and his face lived. He stood up and took a look over the village "well I won't have this view for a while let me enjoy it a little longer", he said forcing a smile, but his cheeks were still rusty from all those running tears.

Suddenly his mind drifted to reality, and it came to him that it was late, and his parents must be worried about his whereabouts. He took out his phone to find it on silent with about fifteen missed calls interchanging from his mother to his father. He looked at his car keys, smiled and said "well USA here we come, as bad as it is that I have to move across the world to study something I don't like, I will be on my own and I will have all the freedom" he laughed headed for the car down the mountain, I can certainly say the spirit of college had finally hit him.

Patience is always the key when trying to search for one's passions and gifts. Just as it was said that everyone comes with a gift, not that everyone must figure it out. Matthew hasn't even lived, yet he already wishes he knew his gifts; I mean he has lived under his parent's bubble they were guiding their dreams onto him and hindering him from having his own. My advice for the young man would be, go out there and live, have patience and you will ultimately find that one thing you can do with little effort, something you can do even when you not expecting payment for doing it, something you can do and escape the world. Patience is virtue.

There he was with his right foot glued to the accelerator headed back home. To my surprise when I thought the young man was hurried back home, he took the long road home. The silver Toyota corolla was flying the streets of Ebenezer. He slowed down by Elsa's home, to his luck he found

Elsa's little brother about to enter the resident, he called him and said "please go and call Elsa for me, tell her it is Matthew" he waited by the gate anxious until thirty (30) minutes later when his smile of relief and anticipation turned to shame and sadness. The boy only went in, and the doors closed behind him, nobody came out. Matthew was still hopeful, and he waited for another 30 minutes with a miserable face while locking at his parent's incoming calls and ignoring them. Whatever told Matthew to wait finally told him to leave, he left like a bat out of hell.

"Here is your camomile tea, it will help you calm down. Stop worrying yourself the boy will come back, he took the car, I am certain he will catch that flight tomorrow. Anyway, tell me, did you manage to talk to the judge about endorsing you for the magistrate position last night?" without paying attention to him, Mrs Nkosi stood up from the bed where she was laying as if she was possessed and pointed to the moving car lights she saw headed their mansion. The Nkosis were well situated in their hill mansion you would swear they carved their mansion out of the hill; they were so up that you could see anything headed up to them, with one way in, one way out. Matthew's car was flying home.

"Is it him?" she asked, and he answered, "of course it is him those sports lights were crazy expensive I can recognize them too well". Both headed to the garage on the speed of light, soon as he got there and opened the garage door, he could see their feet as the garage door was slowly sliding up. By their standing positions he had about eight (8) thoughts of turning back before the door slide fully open, well home is home. Soon as the engine died the silence was awkward and even when Mr Nkosi whispered "do not shout at him" it sounded as though he said it through a speaker, the room stood still, and it was a starring contest at the Nkosi garage.

Matthew took a breath and broke the silence "Mom, Dad am ss..." Mrs Nkosi broke the lock she had up her mouth so fast he did not even finish what he wanted to say, she said "come here boy", boy went, and they hugged. Beautiful as the hug was Mr Nkosi could not hold his horses "Now tell us where you have been"

Mr Nkosi said. Mrs Nkosi let go of Matthew so fast you would swear she had just regained her consciousness from a bad dream. "Uh huh enlighten us Matthew". He stuttered for a good sixty (60) seconds before his mouth could open, yes, I counted! Finally, when his mouth opened, he continued to say, "I was saying farewells to my friends". Whenever Matthew lies, he flinches and for some reason the back of his ear will become itchy.

Both Mr and Mrs Nkosi looked at each other with eyes of suspicion and agreed sarcastically, every fool could tell they did not believe a word he said, but what mattered was he did believe they believed him. "Now let us go finish packing" Mrs Nkosi said leaving the garage and picking the gown belt from dragging off the floor. "So daad" Matthew said with a huge smile on his face hugging his father from behind "is there no way I can get my car faster? Two weeks is a lot for the son of soon to be minister." "Son if that is how you flatter girls, we should be expecting grandkids soon" Mr nkosi said whispering to Matthew, both laughed but their joy was cut short when Mrs Nkosi turned back to say "what!" they both kept quiet, and their grin disappeared. "But seriously son it can take a month or two, so two weeks was the best I could do." The three joked around and packed the night away.

Scene 03

"Leaving home, in a sense, involves a sort of second birth in which we give birth to ourselves"- Rober Neely Bellah

The first cock had not rose yet, and the Nkosis were headed to Cape town international airport. The trip was long and in silence, Matthew had his head by the window looking at the darkness moving backwards as was his mind trying to move back to the past couple of days to see if there was something he did to offend Elsa, when nothing came up his mind would also jump ahead to his awaiting freedom, and he would smile like a kid who got away with stealing sugar.

A while later Matthew was buckled up in a plane, and the engines came to life. He had his headphones on playing (ghost; by Justin Bieber) he did not even hear the plane roar. Smart as Mr and Mrs Nkosi were they could not help but wave to the plane as it got up in the air knowing very well, he could not see them. Matthew continued humming to the song and the plane continued to soar over the mountains and oceans.

Back at the Nkosi residents the folks had the house all to themselves and they felt like teenagers all over again, yet Mrs Nkosi could not keep away from her cell phone. When Mr Nkosi was sneaking on her from behind, he caught her searching "possibilities of a plane crashing" on google and he was immediately hit by shame and guilt of enjoying too much before they could ensure safe arrival of their son. He gently put the handcuffs he had on his hand in his back pocket and hugged her from behind and he gently said, "do not worry yourself mama, Matthew will be fine, we booked him the best flight, he is probably even enjoying, and I will call a friend of mine from the airport to hear about the plane's progress okay!" she nodded anxiously.

Mr Nkosi stepped outside and made the call, Mrs Nkosi was getting more anxious looking at him outside pacing, she was trying to focus on his mouth, and she could not get a thing he was saying. After some countable minutes he stepped back inside with a huge grin and said to her "my love would you just relax, Simon said the plane is well on its way and the atmosphere is perfect, be at ease my love" he said while sitting next to her and brushing her shoulders. "Okay papa I will try to relax" she smiled, and he smiled back at her. He gave her a roguish grin.

"Now come here" he said pointing for her to sit on his thighs. She stood up with so much enthusiasm and sat on his lap, she whispered to him "hold that thought let me freshen up fast I will be back, do not move" she upped and left giving him a wink and he just stood there speechless with his mouth wide open. (shut your mouth dummy! she did not mean you should literally freeze). You would swear he heard me, He immediately shut his mouth and moved across the room, he went to the bar area, where he pulled out a bottle of red wine, a glass and took out a whiskey glass of which he put three ice cubes and a double of scotch whiskey. He went back to where he was seated, like he never moved an inch. He continued sipping his whisky with anticipation losing patience with every second that passed.

Shortly after, she showed up in her pure white silky gown. The gown is just above her knees, he drooled, almost spilled his drink. "Are you going to offer me something to drink?" she asked while approaching him and he went for the bottle of wine without taking his eyes off her. Before he knew it, she was in his face, and she grabbed the glass he was busy searching for with his hand refusing to take his eyes off her. She laughed so beautifully I also drooled "what is wrong with you today, Hunny?" he laughed back and lied "I have never seen you this beautiful" they both laughed, and he continued to pour the wine.

The laughter, smiles and teasing continued for quite some time between the two, for a moment my hope in love tickled. If I did not know any better, I would say the two have been trying to get rid of Matthew for a while. "When last did you dance?" Mr Nkosi asked. Before she could answer he was already up bare foot, holding out his left hand reaching for hers. "Are you serious right now" she asked while accepting his invite, she also slipped out of her slippers and went barefoot. I have never seen such terrible dancers, I guess they just needed to hug and hold each other. In their mind they danced beautifully to (Lloyiso: dream about you).

He took the last sip off his whiskey glass, she took the last of her wine and they starred, as I thought it was a staring contest she advanced towards him, she spread her legs to sit on his lap, covering him with her knees side by side he had nowhere to go. She gently held the back of his head so softly his oxytocin, dopamine and serotonin flew all over his veins. He put both of his hands under her gown sliding and reaching for her back, only to realise she did not have any underwear on but the gown, he lost his mind, his lips immediately got dry, and they kissed. After a moment of passionately exchanging saliva, he tossed her gown down the floor, without any hassles carried her naked to the table across the room and made love like it was their last.

One wise man once said "every morning is a new arrival" the following morning Matthew's flight took its last soar touching down at the Burbank airport. As soon as the engines died, he took out his phone and put it out of flight mode. On the other hand, Mr and Mrs Nkosi were in their bed naked like they both fell from the sky due to their sleeping positions, well they did work each other out. It was around 2h00am when Mrs Nkosi's phone rang, what Matthew did not consider was that his morning was not theirs. Both were deep in their sleep that he left five (5) missed calls, and they did not grab the ringing of any.

Matthew had been in a flight before, but not to a whole different state and alone. When he could not get hold of his parents, he was panicking and scared of getting lost. Not even his joy of being away from his parents could triumph his anxiety. However, he is a smart young man he managed to find a taxi that will take him to campus. He was lucky he only had to carry a small suitcase including of his accessories; he ran the campus for a good two hours looking for the accommodations office which he finally found with a long queue that took him another good one hour to get in.

At the Nkosi residence it was early morning when Mrs Nkosi screamed anxiously to Mr Nkosi as though he literally put her to bed and ensured she miss her son's calls "look, something is wrong I have five (5) missed calls from Matthew" she said while waking him up so violently shaking his chest like she was attempting to wake him up the dead. "Please will you relax and let us call him back and hear from him" he answered her calmly and sleepy. She rolled her huge eyes and dialled Matthew. He smiled to the incoming call of his mother and stepped outside to take it. The three spoke and laughed for a good twenty (20) minutes yet to them it felt like two (2). When he went back to the hall, he was dismayed to see the queue had changed all together and he had to rejoin all over again.

It was after getting his keys to house D, when he realised, he had been going up and down the whole day and his stomach was crying out the loudest. His feet were sore, and it was late to get his luggage delivered from the airport, he could hear belly laughs from the house he was about to go in, excited as he was, none of his expressions could show, hunger and tiredness were swallowing the life out of him. He knocked and the house went silence.

As he was about to knock for the second time, the door opened slowly, and three heads popped up and they immediately went to relieve when they saw a stranger. "And then who are you?" he could not speak any further he just needed to sit down, he went straight inside, threw himself on the couch and opened his mouth "my name is Matthew, and I am your roommate" he said gaping at the opened pizza box that was sitting across the table. "Housemate dummy" one of the boys said and they laughed except

Matthew, he flew across the table to grab the pizza which he stacked the two slices that were left on top of each other and chugged them down his throat.

"Whoa! wait, how many rooms are in here?" he asked with his mouth full of chew. they laughed and Glen said, "there are four room in here village boy, no one will be sharing a room with anyone, how will we entertain the girls?" the three cracked a laugh and demonstrated sex strokes. Well, where are our manners I am Glen, this is Chris, and he is Joel. The boys kicked it up all night long getting to know each other till early hours of the morning. They all went to their rooms and Matthew went to check his, and it was only a bed and a mirror which he stared himself on.

Those couple of hours before the sun could grace them with a smile felt like days to him. He did not have a blanket to cover himself, and he did not want to bother the boys since he knew they went straight to the deep end of their dreams, no lullaby was needed, yet it was for him. Do you know how the wise always say, sit by yourself and you will find answers? Well for Matthew whenever he would try to find answers he would get more question instead. He kept pacing up and down the room taking breaks on the mirror interrogating his reflection on who he is, why is he here, he even started doubting himself if he can even be good at the computer science course he was enrolled in.

The sun started taking a peek bit by bit to the United States, it was like it was shining on his brains when he realized who would be able to calm and comfort him in his anxiety and took out his phone, he dialled Elsa. Of course, it went straight to voicemail but the sound of her voice on the voice mail carried him to bed, and his rambling to her voicemail drifted him to sleep.

As Matthew was drifting in his sleep, he was woken up by the boys to come sign up for his delivery from the airport, it was his luggage, blankets, groceries, just about everything he needed to settle in. Luckily for him the manpower was there, and they helped him set up his room.

"So, you are mama's boy huh?" Chris asked pointing with his eyes to the electronics he had in his accessory bag, it was an apple laptop, an apple tablet, game consoles, extra pair of chargers and besides the bed was a big flat screen that needed to be hanged on the wall. As he tried to answer, Joel pointed to the new clothes and a box of under wears. Before he could answer for himself his cell phone rang, they all cracked a laugh as he was stepping outside to take it "oh mommy misses her little boy huh" Chris commented as he stepped outside.

"How are you settling my boy? Who was that laughing, you made friends already?" Mrs Nkosi asked curiously "mama am okay you do not have to check on me every second, those were my housemates helping me to unpack" "well okay them did the driver also bring the flat screen I asked him to get for you? I hope it is big enough for you to work on" he rolled his eyes and immediately succumbed to guilt "yes ma! I was okay working on my laptop, but the screen will do, thank you very much" "and be careful do not be wooed by city boys, remember who you are and why you are there" "as if I knew" he said to himself just as the call went off.

He went back to the room with a shy smile and found the mess almost out of sight. They were only left with putting the huge screen up on the wall, and that was only because they did not have the tools to. Otherwise, they would be done with it too. The boys were on a roll and not slacking off. Even with his shy smile the room had moved quite far from his shame of being a mama's boy. "Well boys tonight let us show this village fella around campus, plus there is newcomer's welcome party by the common hall" Glen spoke, and he gave a naughty wink. Matthew laughed and said will you boys stop acting like you are seniors here, we all newcomers. Joel threw himself to the conversation with a comeback "but we have walked and known this campus all our lives."

Matthew was hesitant to go to the party, but he knew the mama's boy card was about to overweigh the table. For a change even I found profound joy overlooking Matthew making friends and talking freely as himself without acting to the standard of what is proper for a politician and a lawyer's child. At last, the boys agreed to all go to the party, and they went to their rooms acting all cool, but the excitement on their faces could not be masked as each one was going through their wardrobe trying to find a perfect outfits for the party.

Scene 04

"To be fully seen, and to see. Our hearts jumped together"-Makoko Karabo Lancelot

"So, did you get any feedback from the judge about putting your name up for the magistrate position?" Mr Nkosi asked as he turned to her face with his eyes red and weary like he never caught any sleep. She flinched a bit from his morning breath. Before she could answer he continued to say, "maybe we should call him and set up dinner in some fancy restaurant clearly the party did not work out well." The way she opened her mouth it was clear she was drained off energy and her hope hanging unbalanced "but during the party he sounded so promising" "well then stop giving yourself headache, I heard you tossing and turning all night, and the list of nominees is not out yet, should be out anytime today" Mr nkosi said reassuring her that it was not over until the fat lady sings.

The morning brightened up and gave way to a beautiful sunny day, with only the sunrays giving themselves way to the Nkosi's upstairs porch where Mr Nkosi was relaxed in his short and vest, sipping his 15 years old Glenfiddich. Mrs Nkosi was busy slaving in the kitchen. Mr Nkosi raises his head to the screaming sounds he thought he imagined. for some reason he looked at his whiskey glass with accusing eyes like it was making him hear things. In a moment, his world span normally and he came back to reality to notice it was his wife screaming in the kitchen. He immediately rushed inside, well the immediate of it only applied to him, all I saw was a man who thought he flew like the Flash, but in actual fact the whiskey was weighing on his legs.

Mrs Nkosi had slightly grazed her thumb finger and yet she screamed like she had chopped it off. Fortunately for her Mr Nkosi knew his way around the first aid. He rushed to get the first aid kit from the garage and patched her up. After fixing her up he looked her straight in the eyes with a shame and disbelief look at just how she overreacted to such a small graze. She noticed his look, leaned to him, and embedded her head on his chest. He wrapped his arms around her and kissed her shiny hair.

They stood there for a moment till she calmed down and she raised her finger to have a look, He let go of her and grabbed the finger, he kissed the bandage and whispered to her face "you going to be okay sweetheart" she smiled back at him, and gave a witty laugh "uhm so you expect your one and only amazing wife to cook with an injury?" she asked moving out of the kitchen backwards with a grin on her face. He laughed back "you naughty girl!!" he went around the stove opening the pots checking up on them, she left him no choice.

When the drunk cooks it never ends well, but fortunately for Mrs Nkosi, she knew her husband was an excellent cook, so if he were to mess up, he would not fumble. But the way I see it she might have to stop him from taking another glass otherwise there might a duo kitchen cases at the Nkosi resident, the cutting and burning. But nonetheless there he was so energetic as ever, moving from one pot to the next while dancing to the smooth soul music they were playing.

Mrs Nkosi was served like a queen and they both had a beautiful and tasty feast. Suddenly Mrs Nkosi's energy came rushing and she was all over the dinner table by their porch. The sun was way behind the mountains, it was a beautiful summer evening, hot as hell they were both sweaty, after digging in their plates. "Well, you know the helper is not around on weekends, right? So, this table needs to be cleared Mr" she said trying to maintain a serious face, yet her witty grin could not be hidden. As Mr Nkosi was trying to respond, she lifted her bandaged finger before he could even utter one word out of his mouth. "Okay I will clear the table you run a bath for us" and they both went separate ways.

As much as Mrs Nkosi tried to smile and pretend all is well, at moments she would fail. She stood in the bathroom stared at water wasting away in the bathtub before she could put a stopper in. It was getting late by the seconds, and the magistrate position nominee list was supposed to be out before end of the business day. Her not getting any feedback from the judge was riling her up even more.

Mr Nkosi finished up clearing the table and just as he was headed to the bathroom to join his wife, his phone beeps, when he took a peek, he got fixated to what seemed like a list. he could not read; he kept going at it repeatedly. Mrs Nkosi got impatient and stepped out the bathtub naked as she was "Hunny does it even take a whole year to clear a table for two?" just as she yelled, she bumped into him, and he quickly put his phone away. His staggered face turned into a smile, and both went to take their bath.

On the other end the boys were ready to hit the party. The sitting room was suffocating with different kinds of fragrances and on fire with stylish and elegant outfits. Each one was trying so hard to knot their smiles down their stomachs, yet even a blind man could see their side grins and the nervousness they were all wearing and pretending to be chilled. Although Joel, Chris and Glen were acting like seniors and knowing their ways around campus, the fact was, it was their first time attending a university party.

When Matthew felt out of place and far from home. They had the same feeling too even when their homes were just a few feet away from the campus, as they walked to the party venue admiring seniors and postgraduates pulling up in sports cars, and trending fashions. The boys spend a good hour standing outside by the hall admiring the incoming people, their cars, and clothes, it was worse for Matthew as he saw the kind of stunning girls he thought existed only on Instagram and in movies.

At last, the four advanced with their journey and entered the party. Everything inside was all kinds of awesomeness and more. The party was exceeding their expectations and overwhelming but not to

Chris. Chris was kind of used to the party lifestyle and his cousin was popular and a legend on campus, even though it was Chris's first party on campus it was definitely not his first around town. Through that connection the boys had unlimited access to a bunch of alcohol. The beer Kegels, wines, tequilas, and whiskeys were all for their taking.

The evening wore on, the party was on fire, and the boys chugged beer like it was their final day on Earth. The room continued to swirl until it stopped. And so did the entire universe, or so Matthew imagined. His brain and feeling of consciousness left his body when he spotted the prettiest girl in the room. Everyone else vanished into thin air. He and the girl were having a standoff. Without hesitation, his whole body, directed by his heart, walked right to where she was standing; intuitively, the girl also moved towards him, but just as they came to a stop, she passed and did everything Matthew had imagined to the senior guy who was standing behind Matthew. That was when he realised, he was looking at her and she the other guy.

Everything came rushing back, and the universe came to the end of the pause immediately. The loud music was so irritating to him at that moment, he threw his eyes around the room searching for Chris, Joel, and Glen. His experience had just rendered him sober, his heart became heavier, and his mood went straight to foul. Few moments after he was able to find the boys and he re-started his drinking, only his attention was right where the pretty girl he had a phony moment with was starding with a senior guy she offered a hug and a kiss that were meant for him.

For a moment he was starting to have doubts, when he noticed her looking back at him, He did a good 360° to check and confirm she was not looking at anyone else but him, among his confusion he could not keep his smile to himself, and Joel noticed. "Is that where you had disappeared to when we could not find you?" Joel asked while pointing to the girl with his head. Just as Mathew shied down and trying to answer Joel continued to say "well, I see you player" and they all laughed.

They partied away, fun was had and at last Matthew had stopped gazing across the room searching for the pretty girl his mind was fixated on. They laughed their jaws off, and Matthew turned to go take a leak with his mind still preoccupied to the joke that was cracked and left everyone laughing. He suddenly collided with someone on his fourth step, afraid to look up to who he had bumped into he took a moment watching his drink running down the floor.

When he looked up to apologise, he was faced with the most gorgeous girl he had ever seen so up-close, and this was the same pretty lady he had been eyeing all night, they had a stare. Time stood still and everything around them faded away, leaving just the two locked up in a moment of pure connection. The pheromones had filled up their surrounding and the intensity in their eyes as they gaze into each other's eye was like they can see through each other's soul.

One thing I know about these kinds of stares is that right in that moment you forget all your worries and just focus on the way her lips curves into a small smile and how her hair falls perfectly around her face. You can feel your heart racing and butterflies fluttering in your stomach as you try to hold her gaze, not trying to break that magical moment. It is as if you both are communicating without uttering a single word. It is a look that speaks volumes, conveying emotions that words could never express, and in that instant, you know that she has captured your heart, and you cannot help but wonder if she feels the same way. yes! I do still remember it, even I once had such a feeling of pure unexpected connection.

Unfortunately, the universe could not stand still, till the end of time for them. Time came to resume its course, but that stare will forever be etched in their memories. The world came rushing so hard that soon as he noticed the disco lights in the room and the loud music, his stomach responded to all the drinks he chugged in all night, and he puked on her jacket just as he attempted to rush to the bathroom which he was headed to.

He continued with his walk of shame, double shame to be precise, headed to the bathroom where he spent eternity ashamed of coming out and face his mishaps. Glen, Joel, and Chris were having a caucus on how they should head home as soon as he comes out of the bathroom. The night forgot about him for a bit and went on. Ultimately, he heard the music stopping and he came out to everyone leaving the room. He instantly spotted his house mates and went straight to them; he was sobering up and shivering from the outside breeze and the shame he brought himself.

On their way home he spotted the pretty lady again standing in a group of four and his mind told him to go apologise. When everyone around him was telling him no it was as if they were fuelling his fire up to go there, he went. With one tap on her shoulder, she turned around, before he could even take a peek of her gorgeous face he was met with a fist up his jaws. He could only hear her voice trying to stop the guy from punching him even more, and just as he was trying to catch his balance his housemates swooped in and dragged him home.

Matthew, Chris, Joel, and Glen all woke up to a loud knock on their main door the following morning. Every one of them was reluctant to open thinking they may be in trouble. Chris finally had the gut to open and it was his cousin and a friend with a mini cooler box of beers coming to congratulate the boys on being initiated to their first tertiary rager.

The party continued and Matthew had a resemblance of just how great last night was, his blue eye was getting darker and more visible. Few hours later Chris's cousin left, and they were left on their own tired and slumbering. Chris called them to a circle of caucus where said "well gentlemen classes starts next week so let us finish this week with a banger and grab all the fun we can" as they dissipated to get their rest and ready for the night, Glen mumbled "and tell Matthew to stay away from seniors girlfriends."

"Oh yes, there is that point to raise" Chris agreed with Joel, and he continued to say, "be careful boy, next time it might not be just a blue eye, trust me niggas around here do not play around." Joel and Glen agreed to his statement, each one putting their own opinion on the matter. Matthew had an earful of how he should stay away from girls to stay safe. Finally, the meeting adjourned, and they went to rest.

Scene 05

"The strongest evidence of love is sacrifice"-Carolyn Fry

It had been three days since Mr Nkosi has heard his wife say a full sentence or seen her smile, never mind her teeth. She had high hopes of being nominated for the magistrate position and she had placed it all to the wrong person who disappointed her ineptly. So much as the new year eve party was for Mr and Mrs Nkosi to show off their brilliant son who was about to board a plane to another state to become a brilliant computer guru, for her it was mostly about impressing the judge and convincing him to put her name forward as one of the nominees.

The Nkosis are all about success and prosperity at all costs and Mrs Nkosi was a stranger to failure and not getting her way. This time things did not go as planned, despite her efforts and hard work she was met with disappointment and failure. This unfamiliar feeling has left her feeling lost and dejected. She is failing to come to terms with the feeling of having missed her opportunity to step on her desired position. Mr Nkosi was suffering for it.

He had never seen her so helpless. The night she saw the nominee list it was as though she was looking at her whole life dissipate right in front of her eyes, and he had a front seat view. His heart bled massively seeing her that miserable and devastated, as much as he had influence from his political position, he could not help her, and it broke him. If you were to see her you would not be able to differentiate her from a psychiatric patient. She has not reported to her workplace ever since she found out, and she seemed unbothered. Needless to say, she was a major shareholder in her law firm. I guess that was the reason she seemed unbothered.

"Hunny, you have to get it together please, there will be plenty more and better opportunities for you". Without uttering any word, she turned and looked at him, and he knew exactly what that look communicated, he stepped away from her. It was a week away to the final interviews of the nominees before the best candidate may be chosen for the magistrate position and Mr Nkosi knew he had to get his wife on that list. He did not know how, but he was tired of seeing his wife wither away from stress and feeling of inadequacy. All he knew for sure was that he wanted his wife back. He marched straight to his home office and started making calls.

After hours of calls, all he could get was advice on how he cannot be seen to be involved in this matter, especially under the involved of his wife. Each respond was riling him up so bad that his hands were trembling, and he could not stop stomping his foot under the desk. Finally, he went quiet, did not move and entered into trance state, staring to one side of the wall and his mind was in the works, thinking only what he knew. His pupils dilated so much so that even a layman could tell his thoughts were not pleasant but sinister.

After a moment he finally came back to the living, without wasting any minute he stood up so fast went straight to the door and shut it close, so fast so that when he came back to the desk, the chair he stood from was still spinning. Soon as he sat down, he grabbed a bottle of whiskey and a glass from his cabinet by the desk, he poured in silence, hanged his feet over the desk and started dialling while sipping from his glass. Well, if you know me better by now you would know I stared to have a better look at him as he transitioned to boss mode.

Whatever he gathered from his call, was mixed with high potions of confidence, I hope it was not from the whiskey. But he left his office with his eyes longing to see his wife and he searched for her around the house and finally found her. Sad as her face looked, he had a chin on his face, and he could not hide it. He held her hand and whispered to her, "everything is going to be okay my love, I am going to do everything in my power to ensure that your name is on that list before the interviews day okay!" he spoke so confidently it almost put a smile on her face.

As much as she tried to not be shaken by what he was saying to her. I could tell from her face and how she lit up that she was charmed, and a smile was brewing deep down even though she could not let it out. "What do you have in mind?" she finally cracked her mouth open. She talked with so much eagerness to get a grasp of his plan, and he did not give her the satisfaction "do not worry yourself my love, just prepare for the interview and how you are going to dazzle everyone, do not forget it is going to be live" he said moving away from her because he knew just how persuasive she can be, and he cannot resist her charms much longer.

That one night it stopped raining tears, bitterness, disappointment, and depression at the Nkosi resident, and the atmosphere was finally warm. A little conversation was broken down at the dinner table. she finally ate a handful. "Have you talked to Matthew lately?" she asked. "Not in the past two days when I last called him, I wanted to tell him about your hmmm..." he cut himself before he could remind her of her sorrows "and he sounded kind of busy with his new friends." With an unconvinced face she calmly replied to say, "let us call and check on him right now."

"Hello papa" Matthew answered the phone after a minute of ringing. "Why do you sound like you outside, isn't it even more late that side?" Mrs Nkosi jumped to the call right away and asked. "Uhm I was studying am just taking a little walk to refresh ma'am" he answered with a faint voice and unsure of his answer. Mr and Mrs Nkosi took a moment and looked each other in the eye in despair and surprise "Matthew are you drunk?" they both asked, "no sir, no ma'am" he answered right away before they could finish up the sentence trying to hold his laugh and he could not do a better job, his laugh and ecstatic mood were louder than the words he uttered.

The disgust and disappointment on their faces was sad to watch, but they had their own problems to worry about, than to be brood about a teenage boy being a teenager. Lost for words they just decided to cut the call after a moment of bickering and realizing it was like hammering an empty tin right to their ears considering Matthew's drunk state.

They consoled themselves to the thought that he was just getting to know the place and that classes have not started yet. knowing their son, they trusted that after all the chaos of settling in, when classes start, he will rise to the occasion and make them proud. Even with their anger at ease, nothing could wipe up the disappointment off their faces. "Let us go to bed Hunny, I think I should report to the office tomorrow" Mrs Nkosi said with a doubtful enthusiasm. They both sipped off their glasses and headed straight to the bedroom.

A few minutes after the lights went off Mr Nkosi's phone beeped, he looked and the text reads "found the Nkabi(hitman), I will give you feedback when it is done" he took a deep breath, turned to the side of his wife, and put his arm over her and kissed her good night. "What was that" she asked, and he answered "nothing love, it was just a confirmation of some appointment. "So, you never told me your grand plan about putting me up for the interview" she asked while turning to his side and they went face to face, "like I said do not worry yourself with the details okay, it will be done". Then followed silence and they both went to sleep.

On the other side each day was coming closer to the start of the school year and with each day Matthew and crew were getting more drunk with no care in the world. However, what they should have cared about was their 24/7 loud music. In the early hours of the morning or what seemed to be early hours for them, they were woken up by a fierce knock by the campus securing together with the resident manager. To their luck they were freshman, and they just received their first written warning.

Talking about warnings Mrs Nkosi was also met with a written warning first thing in the morning at work for missing a whole week without a proper reason. Much as she was shareholder she had ranks to report to. Her day back at work started in shambles and that set the tone for the rest of her day as she was trying to fill up all the gabs.

As she had all her focus on the job, Mr Nkosi could not focus at all on his own. His attention was fixated on his phone expecting a call, he was not getting any. He was used to the fact that his influence was vast, and he did not stop to think what he had asked for had nothing to do with his status and it was rather illegal. Impatience was having its stomach full, eating at him.

All Mr Nkosi wanted was to impress his wife and ensure she get her happy ending as he promised her. His office phone rang as he was deep in his worries and his hands were shaking to answer the phone. He answered with enthusiasm and expectation of good news. "My guy told me it is done" the caller said with no greetings nor introduction and Mr Nkosi knew exactly who it was. With a vile smirk he removed the phone from his ear and kept holding it in his hand, deep in thoughts. He could not believe what he had done.

He was awakened by one of his colleagues who fell into his office in a rush and ready to blab. "Have you heard yet" he said without a knock nor greeting, it was as though it is a theme of the day that all of the sudden everyone had lost their manners to greet before going on about their cases.

In doubt and spirit of guilt Mr Nkosi answered "heard what, what do you mean, I did not do anything" his colleagues got shocked for a moment by his remarks but his eager to feed him the news was just way too much for anything to catch his attention "well I hear that Influencer lawyer has been short this morning as she was leaving her house, but fortunately the bustards did not finish their job and she has been admitted to the hospital" "what!" Mr Nkosi replied with so much vile and disappointment in his voice.

"Man, are you sure you are not a cave man? this thing is trending all over twitter there's even a video of the ambulance fetching her, trust me this is going to be a big case" he continued and to Mr Nkosi it was like he pressed mute on him all he could hear was the faint of his voice as he went deep in thoughts and worry. After a short while of what sounded to be gibberish and overwhelming to Mr Nkosi, he finally took the hint that he was talking alone "and you! are you okay Mr?" he asked out of concern when he realized his sad unrattled face and just how his mind was wondering way beyond the mountains.

"No man, I am okay do not worry I just cannot believe the crime in this country, especially on high profiled people" Mr Nkosi finally spoke and put himself together. Both continued with their chat nonetheless, Mr Nkosi could not wait for the man to leave his office and finally the words he had been waiting for came out of his mouth "well let me get back to work" the relief on Mr Nkosi's face was so priceless and he replied to say "please close the door behind you" soon as the door banged Mr Nkosi already had the phone up his ear and a number dialled.

"What did you mean the job is done? Because all you did was give her more ammunition to even win that magistrate post" Mr nkosi asked furiously and with enormous disappointment. "My man am very sorry I just heard but my contact said the security was tighter as a duck's arse, that is the only chance he could get", The phone call continued for a while without finding any amicable solutions and it was all unproductive and a waste of time.

Although it felt like the longest day on earth full of chaos and disappointment for the Nkosis. Finally, nature took its course the sun was nearly at its setting point as the watches stroke the hour of relief. From different locations Mr and Mrs Nkosi were headed to the same destination, as she was driving up the hill to their mansion, she noticed her husband's car following Her's and she drove even slower to allow him to catch up. The garage door slid open for both at once and they parked parallel to each other, soon as the engines died, they opened their windows looking at each other.

The exhaustion was written all over their faces and without uttering any word, each one could see pity on each one's face. Both took a sight ending such a horrible day and they leaned on their seats to relax. Mr Nkosi put on jazz music on a lower volume I admired their moment of relieve, but they had a lot more to deal with. As much as it was just a single day, I could not shake of the feeling that this horrible day may have set a pace for the rest of the week if not for the next couple of months. Soft jazz music and an exhausted mind never disappoints, after a couple of minutes they both went to sleep.

However, no matter how exhausted you are, a comfortable rest is all that matters. Mr Nkosi was first to feel it and woke up in a burst, surprised he had fallen asleep. He looked at his wife still asleep and he began to worry how did their lives come to this. After a moment of worry and admiring his wife asleep he switched off the music, went to wake her up "Hunny I have ordered something to eat lets go inside take a bath so we can rest well" half asleep and half-awake she followed him as he led her inside holding her hand.

They went inside took their bath and soon as they got done Mr Nkosi received a call from the delivery man that their food has arrived which he rushed to fetch and set up the dining table. Their dinner was intense, and they would both steal a look on each other and yet they remained silent throughout. The tension in the Nkosi household was enough to feed the whole village. Mr Nkosi finally broke the silence and asked, "did you hear about Advocate Mahlangu's incident" Mrs Nkosi answered, "yes I have, what a horrible thing to have happened to her" but what was deep in her heart was "I wish she had died, and I got her slot on the magistrate position nominees." But the question that was roaming her mind all day long, that she wanted to ask him but could never find the courage to was "did you have anything to do with it?"

Their little pep talk seemed to have no effect in easing up the tension in the room. Lights went off and both looked opposite sides pretending to be asleep when none of them was able to catch any sleep. After long hours of worries without solutions Mrs Nkosi turned around with her face on the back of his heard. As he was starting to feel uncomfortable and watched, she reached out her hand and spooned him. His mind immediately came to a standstill and before he could figure out the next thing to think of. Her hand started racing up and down brushing his abs reaching just below his waist and up to his nipples.

His breath changed with each lap she took, even deeper and faster as she went slower and slower. His lips became drier with every breath he took, and he would steal a few licks on his lips just as she did on hers. Their eyes went shut and they could see way more than they did when their eyes were wide open. Yet again the silence was broken between the two as they were communicating with their breaths and touches. This seemed to be an effective communication between the two. Mr Nkosi also turned to her side, and both cured their dry lips syndrome. They continued licking off each other restlessly.

They burned off their steam, together with all the tension in the room. The room echoed loudest with their heavy breaths, both trying to catch a breath from all the burnings they had done. Mr Nkosi was breathing heavily with a smile on his face and so was Mrs Nkosi. If I did not know any better, I would say their breaths were in sync. Soon as they caught their breaths, the room went to silent, and they both went to sleep.

It was around 2am when Mrs Nkosi was tossing and turning in her nightmare. She dreamed of herself as the judge of high court but her whole court including the chair she sat on as well as all the benches across the room through to the entrance drenched in blood and she woke as she was creaking a devious laugh in the midst of chaos and blood. Waking up she looked at her husband in a suspicious manner, and she was as convinced as ever that Mr Nkosi was behind Advocate Mahlangu's shooting tragedy.

As much she wishes he had succeeded, her moral values were eating her up. Her conflict kept her up through the early hours of the morning. As soon as the first hen cackled, she was done preparing for the day and by the time Mr Nkosi's alarm rang she was nowhere to be found, as he reached for her in the blankets avoiding waking up to his ringing alarm. In dismay his laziness vanished to thin air, and he woke up and went straight to the bathroom anticipating he will find her in there preparing for the day.

Adding to his surprise he only found traces that she has been there but not her. Took his shower in confusion and when he got done, he called her and she answered, "am sorry Hunny, I left early today I have so much work and it is driving me crazy" He took a breather before he could answer and the only word that could come out of his mouth was "alright", and he cut the call and continued preparing for his day.

Mr Nkosi felt so defeated and out of ideas as to what he would do next to help his wife be placed in that nominee list. He did not know what his next move would be or if it would work, all he knew was he has to succeed in getting her on that list. Stressed as he was, he finally left the house after hours of pacing around like a headless chicken. Soon as he got to his workplace, he found a gathering by the reception area, where most workers were gathered listening to Advocate Mahlangu being interviewed about her attack and how she is accusing the nominees that they were attempting to get rid of her as she believes the Magistrate's role was hers to bag and that they knew they could not compete with her.

Listening to that interview with a wide-open ear he learned an important detail of which hospital she was recovering from, and that seems to have given him a clue to his puzzle. He rushed off to his office and fast as he could he jumped on his elegant chair with a telephone in his hand. The phone was answered immediately, and he whispered "get your man to go finish the job, she is at the Life Bay view hospital" without waiting for an answer he put the phone down anxiously to the sound of footsteps he heard by the hallway passing his office.

His heart was racing so hard like a hammer pounding on concrete, his thoughts were so congested he could not even filter out what had become of him. Not even a look in the mirror could give him answers. Anxiety was slowly befalling him, and his blood pressure rose high. His heartbeat had lost rhythm. Through it all, his ambition and pride to help his wife could not be topped, not even by his health. Each time he would panic he reminded himself just how he want to get his house back to glory and coming home to a happy and content wife. He is willing to risk it all for her happiness and his.

Days passed, and he watched the news constantly, hoping for news about Advocate Mahlangu's demise and there was no mention of her since the interview. Days were getting ahead with his wife giving him looks of disappointment and questioning his promise to her. His contact was not coming through for him and he had to take matters into his own hands.

"Where the hell is this man?" Mrs Nkosi asked herself pacing around the house at 2am in the morning without any trace of her husband and his phone going to voicemail. She wondered herself to sleep trying to figure out his whereabout without any answer other than her own rumbles.

Sleep caught up with her wondering mind, even when she tried so hard to stay up.

The following day she woke up to find him sleeping next to her, he was gawking at her like an owl, she woke to discomfort. He said to her slowly and with a morning voice "I am sorry. I was working late last night, and my phone died" still sleepy and confused she nodded (hmmm) acknowledging his story. Even when she did not believe him entirely, cheating was nowhere near her thoughts. Before she could even come to her senses her phone rang. She answered and immediately went on her focused mode, and her face reactions kept on changing so rapidly and it was not even predictable if she was receiving good or bad news. The call was precise and short in ended in a moment. She put her phone down stared at nothing she was surprised, scared, and overwhelmed.

"Hunny are you okay?" Mr Nkosi asked out of curiosity and concern. She replied, "good news I just made it to the nominee list, bad news Advocate Mahlangu was murdered last night." He feigned surprise and without dwelling to details he congratulated her. "Well, they need me as in now to come and finalise some documents with my nomination and to make it official, so I have to go, I guess" she said still as puzzled and unsure of how exactly she was taking the whole thing nor how to even act regarding the news.

As soon as she left, he let out a huge sigh of relief that he had managed to keep his promise, but at what cost? His joy was clouded with sadness, guilt, and confusion. As much as he was happy, that he will get his wife back and put their name to even greater heights, something in him was broken and he knew his damage could never be repaired. After a moment of self-hate and questioning his morals, he called himself to attention "it is done, and I just have to forget about it, never think of it and take it to the grave, I am a man!" he affirmed to himself.

Mrs Nkosi's appointment as a nominee for the magistrate position came as a complete shock to everyone., herself included. Mr Nkosi was proud of himself to have put her there when her plans to sway the judge to vouch for her had failed. Yet he could not claim the glory considering how he got it done. There is a saying that goes "the end justifies the means" indeed he delivered what he had promised to her, as for the cost it was his to bare. Quick question for you my friend, would your partner kill for you?

Days went by, the magistrate interviews were held, competitive as Mrs Nkosi was, she won. Except she was being dragged and accused on social media that she had a hand in Advocate Mahlangu's death, because she knew she was a worthy opponent. However no negative posts and comments could steal her joy at this moment. She held it by the sharp end and embraced her achievement. You and I know how she got to that position, but fact is it was not her doing and she won the interview fairly. what she needed was a chance and her husband crafted it for her. Her innocence and triumph did not stop the police from investigating Advocate Mahlangu's death, and she was their main suspect and the only person who benefitted instantly from her death.

Scene 06

"Now that I know you exist, how do I not love you."- butterflies rising

California Institute of technology, Pasadena campus was well on its feet and ready to start the academic year when Matthew and his house mates Chris, Joel and Glen were headed to their first classes. As much as the three were well acquainted to the place by now, they could not help it but wake up as though they were south African taxi drivers trying to ensure night shift relievers relieve night shift workers well on time. By the time the sun smiled they were bathed and ready for classes.

(Tick tock, tick tock) The ticking of watches became increasingly audible, as if time itself was slowing down. Each one of them could hear the relentless rhythm of their wristwatches, and their hearts were beating drums lounder than ever. The silence in the siting room was way louder when each one was in their heads fantasizing how their day is going to go about. All the good and the worst that could happen. Just like every new college student on their first day, even they had their legs trembling, and their insides feeling hollow.

When the clock struck 9h30am they picked up their bags as if they were picking up missiles and ready to match to World War 3. Their classes were scheduled to begin at 10:00 AM, each following their individual timetable. As they departed for their respective halls on campus, they exchanged well-wishes for a successful day. Matthew was the last to leave, Locking the main door behind him and he reached for his pocket to get his phone. The gentle California breeze brought him back to reality from his anxiety and fantasizing about the day he was about to step into. He unlocked his cell phone and navigated to his message history, scrolling down to Elsa's messages with the hope of receiving a miraculous response to the messages he had sent since New Year's Eve.

To his demise he found nothing, and to brighten his day he instantly received a text that his car had arrived and ready for pickup. That text did put up a smile on his face and allowed him to forget a bit about Elsa. He carried his smirk across the street and to his software development class. Just as fantasized he got the best out of his first class, it set the pace for him that he was even more confident and ready for his Latin class.

He found his way to the Latin class quick as he could, and he was one of the early birds to the class. His heart skipped a beat both out of joy and shame when he saw the girl he was punched for at his first party entering the room. He could not focus on anything during the entire class because he was too busy trying to sneak glances at her and ensuring she does not notice him.

When the class adjourned, he stood behind, trying to avoid bumping into her at the congestion going out. It was his last class for the day, so he was not in a hurry anyway. To his disappointment, as everyone was near the entrance, he discovered she also stayed behind. She was busy writing in her medium-sized, pouched red book, she did not even notice everyone else was gone.

He stood up to leave the room, she looked up and noticed him. "Hey puke guy" she shouted as he was trying to go as fast as he could to avoid her. He stopped and turned around slowly facing her direction, he cleared his throat and shyly replied "Hii there, I did not see you" he lied, and she replied "Liar" as she was packing up her stationary into her side bag. He had no words to defend himself, he tried to change the topic, and he asked her, "so you are also taking Latin huh?" without an answer she smiled while approaching him and said, "by the way, I forgive you for throwing up on my new jacket and spilling on my new Jordans Damn!" She exclaimed to emphasize her point that she has not received his apology yet.

He felt like he could simply dissolve into thin air, his voice lowered, and shame filled his face as he apologised "am very sorry about that" "how can I make it up to you?" He asked before she could say anything else, lifting up his face and trying to reach for his confidence. She replied "do not worry about it, it is okay and am sorry you got punched" they both laughed as they exited the class.

"By the way I am Matthew" he spoke anxiously as though he was unsure of his name. she giggled and asked, "are you Matthew or are you asking if you are Matthew?" yet another blow his ego and confidence took a knock. He responded shyly and smiling "I am Matthew" "well Matthew my name is Sandra, and please do not say nice to meet you, we already have a history" they both giggled parading the hallway. If you did not know any better, you would say the two come a long way together. "I am sorry again for puking on your new jacket" Matthew said sarcastically. She gave him a side eye and before she could open her mouth he continued to say, "can I make it up to you over coffee?"

He took a deep breath after asking her and so did she before turning to face him.

She unsurely replied "sure". With a smirk on his face "whoa! do not go gangster on me, is that a yes, we can go? Or sure you want to punch me?" he asked jokingly getting back at her for doing the same with his name. she laughed and replied, "it is a date, but can we make it tomorrow, I still have a class to go to and a bunch of stuff to unwrap at my hostel". With so much joy over his face he said, "see you tomorrow then" He left. She stood in one place looking at him walking across the hallway and suddenly coming to a stop. She was so certain he would stop that she could have bet her life on it.

He turned back in a hurry trying to ensure he catches her, only to see she never moved. He hurried back to her and immediately as he approached her, she reached out her hand as he was reaching his phone in his back pocket. No words uttered and she put her phone numbers on his phone, even though they did not have words they both could not keep their smiles inside. She gave his phone back with her numbers saved as Sandra with a red heart emoji next to the name. She turned facing the opposite direction and he moved backwards to the opposite direction facing her with his cheeks to the ears, everyone across the passage could see his molars as he smiled watching her rushing to her next class.

On his way to the commune house, he could not stop smiling, it was even sad to watch, he moved like a mad man. He could not keep his lips together. His mind was only playing at two things, his conversation with Sandra, the way she smiled, and the idea of fetching his car. When he arrived at the house he found Joel already back from his classes. He tried as hard as he can to hide his grin from him, it was just impossible. "And then what is wrong with you?" Joel asked out of concern, when he noticed how Matthew could not put his lips together and how he would get lost in his fantasy world. He gave him a half reason and said, "my car has arrived, so will you come with me to the harbour to fetch it?" With Joel convinced that he was elated about the car, he continued on his happy mood without judgement and the two left to fetch the car.

On their way back Matthew drove like it was his first time behind the wheels. His driving was excellent, pro level to be precise, he was just all excited about the open roads, driving abroad and the adrenalin he felt as he kept on reminiscing his moment with Sandra. With every smile he wore, his leg sticked even harder on the accelerator. The two enjoyed the trip and had a little time to bond and grow fond of each other outside the setting of the whole group. They kicked it like newfound brothers.

Getting lost for directions and using their phone's GPS they finally got back to campus. Upon their arrival the whole crew cheered for him while checking out the car and the sports features that had been installed. It was a bright and chilled evening and the four went for a drive, testing out Matthew's car.

On their way back he finally let it slip and told them he have a date with the girl he was punched for on their first party and that her name is Sanz. "What kind of a name is Sanz?" Joel asked, "oh its short for Sandra" Matthew replied while blushing. "So, you are already on nickname basis, you go player!" Chris commented from the backseat, he smiled while keeping his focus on the road, the boys laughed it out and cheered for him. I bet they wish they had the car during their partying week, well in my opinion, if they did, a lot would have gone wrong, and this was the best time for the arrival of Matthew's car.

Since the new year party, this was the day Matthew was fully happy and genuinely smiling without worrying about Elsa, his career except when he was under the influence of alcohol. He was filled with pure joy and for a moment he was content. However, reality never disappoint, and the night came separating their bonding session, leaving each one on their own to face their different realities. Everyone went to their rooms and this time they actually had something to focus on, the academic year had already started and as first years they had the energy and the excitement to get on with their books. Except for Matthew of course, whenever he had to be alone, my heart ached just as his worries did to him.

There is a saying that goes "life doesn't give you what you want, but what you need" Matthew always consoled himself with these words whenever he would have his anxiety and questioning himself of his purpose, talent and what he want to do. As much as he did not know what he wanted he surely did know what he did not want. Unfortunately for him, it was exactly what he was set up to do. After a moment of worrying and questioning himself he took a look at his programming book, he was relieved to learn that most of the content in there he was self-taught. His guilt for not putting effort in studying was immediately washed away He then needed not to study; he went on his way to text Sandra.

The conversation between the two went on so well that they nearly forgot about the world and lived in their phones for some time. Before they knew it, it was 3H00am and they were not so eager to quit texting, however the body has a mind of its own and they needed to sleep. They had a whole academic day waiting for them the following day and a lot more time to spend together on their date. The thought of their date consoled them to sleep.

Sunrise never disappoint, people with renewed energies were up and ready to take the day head on while the other two with only three (3) hours of sleep were also up and ready for the day. Both Matthew and Sandra brushed their teeth around the same time from their own separate places and it was as though they were looking right into each other on their mirrors, busy fantasizing about how their day would go about. Although they kept on imagining, planning, and wishing for how their day should go about and their date, they knew it was all desires and wishes and that they are in for a surprise. I mean isn't that the beauty of life. Living every next moment as a surprise but still anticipating each coming second to be a sweet miracle. All they have to do is be present and let the day unfold on the heavens commands.

"Life is what happens while you're busy making other plans"-John Lennon

Matthew had an afternoon class, and he took liberty of the morning free to take his car to the car wash. Sandra attended her classes with so much enthusiasm and impatience of getting done with them. The day was quicker to start but the time was dragging, Matthew and Sandra felt it was just against them.

They had not spoken since the day started and they were starting to get sick, and it was not even afternoon yet. Matthew came back to campus rushing to his afternoon class, he passed by the coffee shop they are supposed to meet for their date later on. In passing he wished he could fast forward time and just get in there right at that moment.

Slower as time was, it had not stopped and on his way from class he was headed to the Campus coffee shop in a rush, his class had run over by a few minutes, and he did not want her to think he stood her up. At the top of his breath, he stormed in the coffee shop, for a minute he could not spot her at the corner she was seated writing in her journal with her earpieces on, soon as he noticed her, his face lit up. He sneaked up on her from her behind and he placed his hand on her shoulders, the chemistry between the two is so mighty she did not even have to question who touched her.

He sat next to her and looked deep in her eyes as if just being next to her was not nearly enough, that look spoke volumes and a better interpreter would say he looked at her as if he wished he could be inside of her or her inside of him. However, the world was not theirs yet and they only had to endure with the standard social norms. "I missed you" Matthew interrupted Sandra as she was trying to greet him after a moment of the stare he gave her. She did not get to finish her greetings, but she could not put her jaws together full of smiles and blushing. "Well, you have been in my thoughts too" she finally spoke giggling.

They had long talks, small talks, they laughed and cheered telling each other their childhood stories and the journey they had leading up to that very moment they met. "By the way am I going to get punched if I hold your hand?" Matthew asked indirectly and what he really wanted to ask was if that guy who punched him at the party was and still is her boyfriend. "She giggled and looked him into the eye and asked, "Matt are you jealous?" Without hesitation he answered confidently "yes I am" that was not the answer she had expected, she knew he was, but she expected him to do a run around about it, shocked and out of words as she was, she looked into his eyes and saw every bit of that "yes I do" and she knew he was dead serious.

After a moment of awkwardness, she finally had some words flowing into her mind and broke the ice she said "no sir you will not get punched, that was just one of my brother's friends he was trying to hook me up with, you have nothing to worry about and I put him in his place" she said assuring him like she was assuring a scared baby that monsters are not real. I am not certain if he did comprehend any other word she said after "no sir you will not get punched" he swiftly moved his hand and put it on top of Her's, on the coffee table and he said, "I have been dying to tell you that you look so beautiful, and I want to kiss you so bad".

Dark skinned as she was if you looked closely, you could see her face turning red, her pupils dilated and suddenly she felt a rush of sweat coming down her forehead and behind her neck, she squeezed her legs together putting one top of the other responding to the tickling she felt in between her legs. Right in that moment she knew her heart and body were failing her. She tried so hard to act content but from that moment she failed to look into his eyes throughout their continued conversation.

"So, computer science huh? Are you some kind of a nerd or genius?" she asked trying to get out of the intense conversation and he replied, "well I would not say genius but that is all I know and good at" he exclaimed, and she saw right through his sadness and frustration all over his face when he said, "that is all I know". He continued to ask, "what about you?" "Well, I am a words girl and all I want to do is share my stories, inspire and motivate the world" she said confidently, and it hit him hard to see someone so enthusiastic about what they do and doing what they love. The next conversation was all a blur to him, he was in over his head worrying about his own path. She noticed this topic had put him on the edge and she said to him "there is a place I want to show you."

Without wasting time, they both stood up, he held her bag to his car. He drove, and she gave directions. Finally, they arrived to what seemed to be a park, rather a private park I could say, except it was not private it was just on the side of campus that most people do not reach. The park was greener, beautiful, and so colourful. Just across the edge was a small lake and a wooden bench right at the perfect view of the lake. They parked near the bench and took a sit there. Matthew could not take his eyes off the surrounding. I could say this was the one time he was around Sandra, and he could manage to look elsewhere besides her pretty face.

He was mesmerized by the beauty of nature. Sandra did not realize she brought him there to be taken by nature from her. Seated on the bench she caught his attention by putting her hand on top of his hand that was placed on the bench in the space between the two. It was as though she performed CPR (cardiopulmonary resuscitation) on his snatched soul, he immediately came to life to realize the dime he had next to him. They looked at each other and filled the gap between them in an instant, moving towards each other swiftly.

Everything besides them blurred and they only had each other. They closed on one another so swiftly you would swear they were being pulled by the world's strongest magnets. He looked into her eyes, he saw peace, she looked into his she saw adventure and confusion. There is a saying that "when you are in love you know." They did not know, yet every part of their body was telling them otherwise.

The grip they had on each other's hands tightened as they met with their foreheads and lost sight of each other's eye when the butterflies in their stomachs propelled them to close their eyes. However, they could feel the heat of the burning flames in each other's heart. They did not have a view of each other especially with their eyes closed but it felt like the perfect view they ever had of one another. Looking down into one another's soul the magnets in their lips could not hold off any longer as they breathed heavily down each other's throats, they kissed.

That was a beautiful scene to watch, even I felt my heart melt, Everything I ever read in fiction of what an amazing kiss looks like, I saw it and for a moment I felt it, and I knew it is not all lies. A kiss so passionate I could not hold off my tears. I felt my heart rejuvenating and ready to experience love once more. Whoa! be patient with me, I am looking trust me! just between watching over Matthew's journey and my own trust issues it is hard but am doing my best. So, relax perhaps next time you will hear about my own love story, and it is going to blow your mind up.

As much as they liked and loved the kissing and living in each other's arms reality was real and they could not hold their breaths forever. At last, they had to let go of each other. After a long pause Sandra broke the silence and said, "well this is my favourite place to clear my mind and write" she turned and looked down the lake, he also turned looking down the lake, leaning himself to the bench he replied to her "this a beautiful place, thank you for showing it to me, so what inspired you to write?" he asked.

She went on to explain what inspired her writing, but he was on his phone taking pictures of the sunset by the lake's view. She went on and on blabbing and he went on and on snapping. She stopped for a moment in realization of how happy and passionate Matthew was in his quest of taking pictures. She sat back and watched him moving from one end to the other getting his snaps from flowers to portraits of the sunset and to finally asking her to pose for him.

Matthew was so excited he did not even realize it, but she saw a person so passionate, invested and enjoying his craftsmanship and he was just playing around like he usually did from the moment he owned a smartphone. Most often your talents and passions are right in front of you without you realizing them and yet waiting for their banger entrance. Matthew had his all this while and he kept on bypassing it while searching for it, luckily for him on this day Sandra saw it for him, and she was not about to keep quiet about it.

Finally, he tired, and dusk was upon them, there was no more sufficient light for taking pictures. They reverted back to the bench where she was teasing him saying "Mr photographer let us see those snaps" he sat down his breath was so high and loud you would swear he was doing hard labour. She put her legs on his lap and adjusted herself to be closer to him, she could hear his loud breath and his heart beating fast she put her hand on the back of his neck and kissed him. In a moment, his heart was beating extremely low his breath was back to normal, he felt an ease.

"What kind of magic was that? He asked and she repeated, she kissed him again to shut his mouth. It worked again he shut his mouth and took out his phone to show her the pictures. They went through the pictures, and she was impressed. What she saw was extraordinary and she could not even begin to fathom why people are not paying for such talent. "You are really talented" she said and paused for a moment to look at him and see if he really grasp the talent she just noticed, and he seemed to not be grasping it.

"You said earlier that you did not know what your talent is right" well this is it, talent coupled with passion" he paused for a moment and replied, "you think?" "Dude! have you seen how your face lighten up when you take pictures? If that is not passion, then I do not know what is" she said confidently and continued to say, "people sell these kind of pictures for a fortune and you sleeping on your talent, stuck up in classes you do not even like nor enjoy." He tried to act casual, but the words really hit him hard, and he began to reassess the path he was sliding down on.

They could no longer take on the evening breeze and they moved to the car. Sandra still glued to Matthew's phone checking out the pictures. There was a vast of them to go through even from back home, From flowers, sunsets to his car and everything nature. Matthew saw he stand no chance of grabbing her attention and drove to the nearest McDonalds just outside campus and she did not even realise she was outside campus, until he asked her what she wanted to order at the drive though.

They ordered and headed back to campus, and she continued scrolling till she got to the previous year's pictures. She came across a lady posing almost identical to how he had directed her to pose for him. She felt her heart turn cold and fast, her head becoming dizzy, and she suddenly became full. But she is a brave young woman, and she did not mention a thing, yet she did say "well it is late, and I have some work to get done, please drop me at my place". She directed him, soon as they arrived, she jumped out of the car so fast, when he tried to run behind her she was way ahead, she entered the hostel's main entrance, and she knew he could not follow her inside that late. Boys were not allowed inside after 19h00.

In his confusion and the demise of his joy, the only thing he could do was to drive away and try to call her from his place. He drove with his mind wiggling around the situation trying to figure out why she stormed out of the car like that and finally he got to his resident, where he found the boys playing in the sitting room and joined them. In a moment he realized he was not even paying attention to the boys and his mind was trying to do a playback. He excused himself to his room where he wanted to call her, and he realized he had left his phone in the car.

He went to get his phone from the car, he unlocked it to realize she had reached on pictures of Elsa where she was posing for him taking picture of the sunset at the Zwart-berg mountain back at home. Finally, he understood her tantrum and realized she was not just being woman, she actually had a reason behind her sudden change of mood and frustration. He could not go back inside, he drove to her hostel, he parked right by the front door and called her. Well, she ignored the first sixteen (16) calls and with his persistence she got annoyed and answered the seventeenth (17th) one. He was not sure if it was another voicemail and soon as she breathed, he heard her breath and felt the pain in her deep breaths and silence.

"Listen what you saw is not what it looks like, and if you could come out, I can explain better" he spoke so fast with his voice shaking and she hung up. She stood up from her bed and saw his car parked down front through the window and she had no intentions of doing down there. He called one more time she did not answer. Few seconds after she heard the car start and looked out the window, she saw him drive away. She stood there looking at the Campus lights and collecting her thoughts when she saw him driving back and he parked right at the same sport.

Matthew stepped out of the car, and he stood at a spot where he was able to see her from the window and where she could clearly see him. He took out his phone, he texted and waved his phone to her as a signal to have her check hers. She stepped back to take her phone from the table and the text reads "I know I messed up; I am sorry and if only you could give me a chance to talk to you, you might get my story. And by the way I went to fetch my blanket in case you do not come out because there is no way am going to catch any sleep at my place knowing you angry at me" soon as she finished reading the text, she threw her eyes out the window and there he was kneeling and begging her to come out.

"Get off the floor, you embarrassing yourself" That was the text he received back, and he felt his heart shredding but nonetheless he was standing on business; not going anywhere until he has talked to her. In a moment she closed the window together with the curtains and he just stood there in dismay. Few moments later the light went off and that is when he knew she was not coming, he went to the car tilted the seat and laid down. It was fairly late, almost midnight and sleep caught up with him.

As he slept thinking, she had also slept peacefully what he did not know was she was moving in the darkness taking peeks at the window trying to see if he leaves. She threw herself to bed trying to convince herself that she does not care, and he can sleep by the car for all she cares, yet time proved she was only lying to herself. As he was snoring in the car, she was tossing and turning without catching any sleep for hours. She was surprised when she grabbed her phone to see what seemed to be 10 minutes to her had been four hours.

It was 4am when she decided she needed closure. She put a gown on top of her pyjamas and headed downstairs, straight to Matthew's car in fury. For some reason she was blaming him for her lack of sleep. She stood for a moment looking through the windscreen watching him sleeping and she got even more furious. She gave a bang for a knock, and he instantly woke up.

He was happy to see her and terrified at how her face looked and the anger she portrayed. He opened for her, she got in, looked straight forward, folded her hands to her chest and went mute. He was just as surprised, and he spoke "Sandra" she did not answer, and he said it again this time trying to touch her. She slowly unfolded her hands and gave him one hot slap to wake him up, in her mind that was for costing her, her sleep and creativity.

The two went on bickering and shouting at each other, and before they knew it the campus had come to life and people started moving around. It seemed they had not resolved their issues yet and they could not continue their nonsensical fight in light of people. Sandra grabbed the door to open it so she can leave, Matthew grabbed her other arm so fast that when he pulled her inside the car, the door shut from her opening hand, and she almost collided with him. She looked straight into his eyes and he straight into hers and she understood she was not going anywhere. He started the car and drove out of campus.

They drove for hours in the middle of nowhere, headed God knows where. It was 10h00am when they came across a filling station and a motel by the side of the road, and they stopped. She was still in pyjamas; he went up the motel booked a room and came back to grab her from the car. She was so embarrassed to move around in pyjamas this time of the day in the middle of nowhere. Without even communicating he knew she was embarrassed he took her to the room, ran a bath for her and as she went to take a bath he went out.

In no time he was back with breakfast and a dress for her. It was a beautiful short black dress with a cut on the side and she smiled to herself on the mirror looking at how beautiful she was in it and how it was a perfect fit. He went in the bathroom as she was still on the mirror to take a bath, and he said to her "the food is getting cold" he spoke in passing as he was undressing to take a bath. She continued doing her hair like she did not hear him. In a moment she was done with her hair, and she started putting some of his lip therapy on her lips long enough for him to realize she was peeking at him bathing through the mirror.

Soon as she realized he noticed; she went out of the bathroom. She took out the food from the bag and set up a table for two putting each one's food side by side. He could not believe his eyes when he came out of the bathroom to notice she had also waited for him. She was busy scrolling on her phone and soon as he sat down at the table, she put her phone down and it was like they were in sync; she closed her eyes and so did he, she prayed "God bless this food before us as we are about to eat" and they both said "amen" at once.

They continued to eat in silence you would swear they were table mannered. After a few bites they both could tell the tension in the room was not doing justice to either one's appetite. Matthew took out his phone and went to the pictures he took of Elsa posing for him, he marked them all, stood up from his chair and went to stand behind Sandra. He put the phone on the table in front of her and he said, "look this is a past chapter in my life that I am way past, and I should have deleted it" he then pressed the delete key.

"Do you think I am stupid?" she said turning from the chair and looking right into his face. Before he could answer she stood up beside him, he was looking down on her and she was looking up at him. "don't you have a past?" he questioned her with his voice raised up. A little bit of anger eased up from her face and she came to a calm state where they were able to talk and biker in a civilised manner.

"Look I like you; I liked you from the very first time I laid my eyes on you; I was under the influence but the sight of you not only numbed my body but my heart and soul." He took a breath and continued to say "That moment I finally felt what Romeo felt and I knew right then and there that I had found my Juliet" he knelt and continued to say "please be my Juliet" a tear dripped down her left eye and she knelt with him, they simultaneously grabbed each other's hands. "So, what did you want to do to me when you first saw me at that party and puked at me?" she said the last part jokingly trying to break the ice and he let go of her hands and grabbed the back of her neck locking his hands and he slowly drew her closer to him, she could not breath no more.

She leaned her mouth for a kiss, and he went for her ear and whispered, "I was imagining you naked" his whispering voice rendered her numb and horny she could not even put a smile as much as she tried to fake a laugh. She pulled back her ear to kiss him and he passed the mouth again and went for the other ear and whispered, "will you be my Juliet?" "Hhhhhh ye yes!" she finally spoke out loud, and he finally let her kiss him.

They kissed so passionately for minutes, and the hormones were flying so high in the room they could not control them no more. They stood up at once without getting off each other's throats, and he carried her off the floor and took her to bed. After a moment of kissing and undressing, he whispered to her let me look for condoms and she exclaimed "ye yes! hurry" at the top of her mute voice. He looked everywhere in the bathroom he could not find any and he put on his jean and shirt like a hurricane went past the room and went to the filling station downstairs to buy condoms with a furious face. He was busy whispering to himself "what kind of a motel that does not keep condoms in the room?" Unfortunately, he could not get any answers.

Without wasting time, he came to the room and to his surprise Sandra was dressed up and fixing her hair, she seemed to be in distress. Soon as he walked in on her she noticed him and said, "Matt we have to go right now!" he knew she was not angry at him when she called him Matt, but he could not figure out why were they supposed to leave so sudden. "Why what did I do wrong now?" he asked out of concern, and she replied "it is not you, I missed literature class, and the lecturer is kind of my mom's friend, and she reported me that I was absent" he looked for his keys and the engine roared straight back to campus.

They got to campus, and he dropped her at her hostel. She needed to rush to her next and last class of the day she had, and he went straight to his room. He found Joel in the sitting room relaxed he had finished his classes for the day "Bruh where have you been? You never came back last night after you came here and stormed out like a maniac" Joel asked soon as he stepped in, and Matthew replied, "well you will not believe this but worry less, let me tell you all about it." He laid on the couch with his feet rested on the table and told Joel all about his night and morning.

Matthew missed an entire day of classes, and he was unapologetic about it. No one could wipe the smile off his face. When he woke up from his nap, he found that Sandra had texted him and requesting to see him, it was around 19h00 when he went to meet up with her and brought her back to the house. He entered the house and heads turned as Matthew and Sandra were headed to Matthew's room.

They got to the room and they both sat on top of the bed like strangers, followed by a little moment of awkwardness until Sandra asked, "are you not going to offer me anything to drink?" "Oh yeah let me get you something to drink" he instantly upped and left the bedroom; he went straight to the kitchen to prepare a snack for the both of them. He put out a stray where he put various snacks and fruits on, two bottled water and a litre of juice and two classes. He did all that with Chris, Joel and Glen hovering on his neck trying to mock him that he is trying to impress the girl and how they never thought he would be the first to bring a girl to the house when they met him and that he is doing well for a village boy. They laughed and continued with their jokes, and he hurried back to his bedroom.

When he entered the room, he noticed that his disco lights were turned dark red and as he looked up, he could not believe his eyes. what he saw snatched his breath away and he felt his hands shaking until he reached for the table to put, the tray he was carrying. There she was in a beautiful sexy black lingerie, and she said "well you wanted to see me naked right? I figured earlier we were up on each other you could not see properly" he drooled, and he unconsciously approached her. He could not feel any part of his body, he blinked, and the spirit of desire took over his body. He slowly gravitated towards her against his will.

Before he could get closer to hold her, she reached for his hand and directed him to sit on the chair she had placed at the centre of the room beside the bed. He sat there and she shushed him, putting her finger on his lips. She reached for her phone and played slow chilled soft music. Before he could catch a breath, she gave him a lap dance. His heart was racing so fast his face became sweaty and his whole body turned red. Finally, he could not take it anymore he stood up as fast as he could. like he was in a hurry, and he grabbed her by the waist, she fell right into his arms. They teared each other apart until they threw themselves on the bed to rest up, she laid with her head on his chest. Before they knew it, they were fast asleep.

Scene 07

"Chaos is the fertile ground from which creativity springs." -Unknown

Days went by Matthew and Sandra have been enjoying their newfound relationship with no hassles, being each other's Romeo and Juliet has never been that amazing. Besides going to classes, they were not allowing anything else to separate them. "Tell me, what is stopping you from following your passion. if this course drains you like this?" Sandra asked Matthew while they were chilling in his car. "And do what sell pictures? My parents will never allow that" he replied to her with a sad tone, and she looked back at him with pity.

"Don't be afraid to give up the good to pursue the great"-John D. Rockefeller

"What about you? What do you want?" she asked him and continued to ask, "do you want to be this miserable for the rest of your life?" he did not have any words to respond to her and he deflected by saying "today I am the one choosing a movie, we cannot watch romance everyday" she noticed his deflection and played along she said "well, don't you love me every day?". Her face turned wider when she realized she had spoken out loud the L word, she looked so shocked and so did he. Their shocked faces birthed an awkward silence, and it lived for a moment.

"Well yes I do, I love you every day, always" and he took a deep breath anticipating her reply to the declaration he just made. She looked him in the eye with tears far withing her eyes, as her eyes slowly turned watery, she kissed him and said, "I love you a lot Matt." The love between the two was so passionate, revitalizing it was a sight for sore eyes. It has only been two months since they started dating and you would swear, they had known each other for decades. Well, if they were to ask for my advice, I would say this relationship was sudden and moving fast, but then again that is just me, with my loveless opinion.

Matthew received a call as they were chilling in the car, The caller said "check the link I sent you" it was one of his old classmates from high school and as he opened the link, he saw his mother on the front page of the local newspaper being accused of the murder of Advocate Mahlangu. As he stared on the phone trying to read the article, Sandra was busy trying to ask him "what is going on" he ignored her until he finished reading the article, and he took a big sigh while handing her the phone to see what is going on.

"Is this your mother?" she asked, and he faintly replied "yes." She continued to ask, "do you think she did it?" "My mother is many things, but she is no murderer" his voice came out so unsure and he was worried about his mother. He took his phone back from Sandra and dialled up his mother, they spoke for a considerable amount of time, and she assured him not to worry, she had nothing to do with the allegations and she will soon fix the situation. Even when he did not believe her fully, her words soothed his heart from worry.

Matthew's birthday was coming in two days, he and Sandra distracted themselves from the article by trying to discuss his wish list. As they were busy debating and cheering, a car parked besides them, they were inside the campus yard, so they did not worry nor pay attention to it. Until the guy who parked got out of his car and headed towards them. "Sh*t that is my brother" just as she ended that sentence, he knocked on the passenger door where she was seated. When she opened the window, he said nothing more than "get out."

She got out and got scolded for not sleeping at her hostel, gallivanting with Matthew, how she could get hurt, how it could hold her back on her studies and how college boys are good at breaking hearts. Well, if I had a say in that I would say funny how he wanted to pass her to his friend and now he catches smoke when she is with another guy, who is probably less harmless than a senior, unfortunately it was not an issue for me to get involved in. However, it was as if he was talking to a stone, she did not listen to a thing he said, but she knew she had to leave with her brother, she went back to Matthew's car grabbed her bag and phone and she took a ride with her brother who dropped her off at the hostel where Matthew picked her up a few seconds later.

They had a good movie night, being all romantic and playful. They were just so overly happy except Matthew had a worry at the back of his mind about his mother. They ended up reverting back to the issues of Matthew's birthday wish list, he rambled and ended up not saying what he really wished for. She looked around his room and realized he was not lacking anything, anything but purpose. She did not know how to get him purpose, but she knew she was going to do something about it.

Back home in the mountains of Western Cape at Ebenezer trouble was brewing for the Nkosi family as the local police invited an abroad crime analyst and investigator to look into Advocate Mahlangu's murder. The community was riled up and demanding justice with the hashtags of (#no one is above the law and #justice for Adv Mahlangu). Mr Nkosi was right to fix his wife's dilemma, he was right to want his wife back to happiness, but he swallowed more that he could chew by having a high-profile advocate murdered.

The Nkosis were making front pages day after day. While Mrs Nkosi was innocent and trying to figure out where all these allegations come from, Mr Nkosi was busy trying to use his political powers to have every article about the Nkosis taken down. He even resorted to threatening journalists and bribing some. What he did not understand was that the masses were tired of watching high profile families getting away with a lot of crimes, and his family was made of a Politician and a Magistrate. The masses wanted to make an example of them.

The articles kept on being written, the tweets kept on trending and finally the Investigator was onto something. Mr Nkosi was backed into a corner watching his entire world crumbled right in front of him. They could not even step outside their mansion without having the paparazzi on their faces. One evening as they were consoling each other and planning a trip away to catch a breather, the hired crime analyst and investigator knocked on their doors with two other South African police officers by his sides.

"Good evening, I am Mr Murray, crime analyst and investigator, how are you doing sir" he spoke immediately when the door slid open. Mr nkosi opened the front door looking surprised and frightened at once. He greeted back and Mr Murry reached for the envelop from one of the officers accompanying him, he handed it to Mr Nkosi and with it he said, "please do not make any travel arrangements outside the country" he took a pause and continued "be safe sir and Mam" he saw Mrs Nkosi coming to stand behind her husband.

It was at that moment Mr Nkosi realized the grave he had dug up for his family, their reputation, and the name they have worked so hard to build. Even when he knew what he did could not come back to haunt him personally, he could not bear the thought of it happening to his spouse. Mr Nkosi prepared for this moment should it arise, but it was at the expense of his wife. It was getting less and less burry to him that he has to sacrifice her if he was going to salvage what was left of the Nkosi name.

That night he waited out for Mrs Nkosi to sleep, and he slipped out a disposal bag from his secrete safe in the study room. He went to her car, opened the boot, and slipped the content of the disposal bag just under the spare wheel. This was his last resort and desperate move he had to make. He felt all the walls closing in on him, but he could not lose his name and reputation.

The following morning Mr Murray managed to crack the damaged hospital CCTV footage, with help from anonymous who was just being a good citizen, and his case just got easier. Right after that he called the car tracking company where he confirmed Mrs Nkosi's car was near the hospital around the time Advocate Mahlangu was murdered. Without further ado he went to the Nkosi resident with two warrants, one for the arrest of Mrs Nkosi and one for Searching their premises.

When Mr and Mrs Nkosi saw the police vehicles from the balcony, they knew they were headed for them, and it was not good news, the police cars were flying up the hill. To their arrival Mr Murray described one of Mrs Nkosi's dress as "royal blue, long with long sleeves" and he asked her where the dress was. She replied "in my wardrobe" with such high confidence, but to her surprise when she searched for it, she could not find it anywhere. Next, she was presented with a search warrant, and they turned the Nkosi resident upside down until they found the dress in her car boot under the spare wheel.

Her shocked face was so priceless, she even felt like this was all a very heinous nightmare. The discovery of the dress was followed by a warrant of arrest. In the midst of her confusion and agony she noticed her husband not so shocked and the look she gave him as she was being cuffed and sent to the police vehicles was so disheartening and she was disgusted by him. Her heart crumpled in pieces to her thoughts and realizations. She cried until no tears could come out anymore and she could not utter a word, her face so red and swollen the universe had knocked her out.

The police ensured to arrest her late at night so they could avoid the paparazzi, and as much as the Nkosis were in the wrong, their impact on the country was undeniable and as such they deserved the respect. The state could not afford to blindly put them in the lion's den with the media. The following morning was the morning of Matthew's birthday and the news of Mrs Nkosi's arrest was moving around the community as rumours.

On the other side Matthew was being served a nice and yummy, delicious breakfast in bed and he was all smiles as Sandra was singing a happy birthday song for him. He was having a time of his life when his phone rang from his father, who announced to him about the arrest of his mother. His heart shattered like glass against a concrete floor. He was devastated he became full and numb, even when his father assured him, that he will get her out his hope was suffocating.

Sandra tried to cheer him up by giving him his birthday present earlier, unfortunately It did not bring much light to his darkened shallow face. His birthday gift was a quest, and he did not have any energy. She tried by all means to take his mind over the issue of his mother's arrest and she saw it in his phony smile that she was failing dismally. she left him to go about his quest while she heads to class.

He went on about his quest with as much minimal energy as he could pour to it. It took him nearly three hours to put together all the clues that were in his room and he ended up driving to one of the Art galleries in town. In his tiny brain it was just any other gallery but in fact it was one of the best in the united state and Sandra knew it. Soon as he introduced his name to the receptionist, she knew exactly who he was and what he came for.

Without wasting time, she directed him to the golden corner where they hanged all the priceless portrait and paintings. There was a mini table, and a chair placed by the corner, on top of the table was a shoe sized box wrapped in a red ribbon. When he saw the box, he knew he had completed the quest, and it was time to get the price.

He sat there for a few minutes admiring, anticipating, and guessing what awaits him in that box. Little did he know that box was a ticking time bomb about to blow his life forever. Sandra was not around to see this sight and to finally see him not worried about his mother's arrest or anything in the world but just admiring the art that hangs around him and only worrying about the mystery box in front of him.

His curiosity got the better of him, his courage filled up the room, he finally untied the ribbon open. His heart went loudest and faster as he slowly took of the lid off the box. Inside the box was three items Sandra had figured Matthew needed, was she right? We are yet to find out. Inside the box was an elegant vintage camera, a book named (The alchemist) this is one of the best rated books, it talks to oneself about following their dreams and passion. Last but not least was a tape written on it (cat burns: live more and love more).

Matthew was having mixed feelings about his quest price and birthday gift; he did not know what all these meant for him. However, that did not stop him from taking his time admiring the camera and wondering how she figured out it was one of his all-time favourite. He packed everything back in the box, ready to go and start exploring. When he lifted the box off the table, he noticed a small envelope underneath the box written Matthew in bold letters on it. He opened and it reads:

"Take a look around you, I mean really take a look, the best gallery in the state, right? but guess what! Somehow, I believe you can do much better than what you are looking at. Live while you live and live for you. Be the best you are meant to be. Happy birthday"

His smile went from ear to ear, his head lifted up and he walked out with an enormous confidence. Soon as he entered the car, ready to drive back, reality kicked in and his head was blowing up trying to choose between his and his parents dream. His parents sent him halfway across the universe so he would return to them as one the best computer scientists in the world. He had the responsibility to grow the Nkosi name to even greater heights, a seed planted by his parents.

He had the talent to grow the Nkosi name to even more greater heights, but his talent was not considered an honourable way to excel according to the society's norm. Back in the villages art is not appreciated until it is a proven means of income and influence. The Nkosi Family was made up of a politician and a lawyer (newly magistrate) and he knew they would not take an artist never mind a mere photographer. Matthew was faced with a hard choice to make, and it was clear to him that he owed himself satisfaction and self-fulfilment, yet he did not wish to disappoint his parents.

He flew the streets of California headed back to campus manoeuvring through the traffic like a mad man. He was up in his head failing to solve his agony, failing to choose himself, failing to choose his parent's dreams. He had a dream of his own. His feelings were heightened to the tape he was listen all the way through on repeat. He was listening to his gift tape, and he knew he had to live more, he owes it to himself to please and be true to himself.

This sight of Matthew battling with himself was not pleasant to watch, yet it was a sight perfect for a beautiful story and a fight worth the fight. I would name the story (Matthew's dilemma) and say Matthew was trapped in a maze of indecision, his parents with unwavering conviction, envisioned a bright future for him in Computer science, a path they believed would bring both prestige and security. Yet his heart yearned for the vibrant world of art, a universe of creativity that ignited his soul.

Matthew was caught between the weight of parental expectations and the pull of his own desires, He found himself paralyzed, and indecisive. The conflict within him grew bigger, casting a shadow over his bright and delightful day as he struggled to reconcile his parent's dreams and his own aspirations. It is thanks to the God and Gods he managed to get back to his room unscathed from all the near accidents he ducked. However, his head was scathed the hardest, he did not know whether to thank his girlfriend Sandra or to despise her for the misery she caused him.

It was early hours of the evening, and he continued drowning in his indecision and admiring his new camera when his phone rang, he answered and heard "Happy birthday my boy" he took a moment of silent he could not believe his ears. "I hope you are having a good day there and not planning crazy parties" his mother continued to speak despite his silence. He giggled and said, "how! what happened?" she replied, "well I may be down, but I still have some influence, I made bail soon as I got in, my trial will start next month." He was elated to hear his mother's voice especially to compliment the day he just had.

They both needed that conversation after the day they just went through, it was refreshing and hopeful for both of them. She could tell he was not at his happiest and he could tell something was eating her up and it was not just her arrest. How do you tell your mother that all the plans and investment she made for your future were in vain? how do you tell your son that his father is a murderer who framed his wife? It was a stalemate between the two and they could not share their bothers, they just said their goodbyes and wished each other well.

Matthew stepped out of the room to go chill at the lounge with his house mates who wished him a happy birthday and asked him if he wanted to go clubbing to celebrate, he turned them down without even a shred of interest. They made a braai and just chilled indoors, everyone who had a glimpse of his face could tell he had a story to tell. All he wanted was a space where he could not be alone. Sandra was busy finishing up her poetry project, and he could not wait for her call. He knew she was his peaceful place.

At last, she called, he stormed out like a hurricane to fetch her. She was his safe place and the only confidant he had. He did not know exactly what he needed from her to help cool his head but at this point he knew she always knows just what he need and this day he was up to test her if indeed she could be his escape. Sandra is a free spirit, she has a good family who support her and her aspirations, she was studying and doing what she loves, the two were directly different, yet together they were inseparable like magnets.

He jumped on her with a hug soon as he had her in the room. She had also missed him painfully; she had not spent that much time away from him since they became inseparable in the past weeks. His breath slowed down as his arms squeezed her tiny fit body tighter. She could feel every part of his body up against hers. She had one arm on his back and the other on the back of his neck. She felt his manhood poking her belly button as she slowly rubbed the back of his neck with her pointy artificial nails.

She took her head off his chest looked up at him and like magnets their lips attracted, they kissed. After a moment of kissing and touching she reached inside his trouser and she could feel his disappointment and shame when she noticed his erection was down. His identity agony together with his family issues were fuelling him up and it was not helping for him to have one more thing to worry about. Just as he expected she knew exactly what he needed "do not worry, it happens to the best of us, and the stress does not help, lay down let me give you a massage and let us ease up that tension" she said with a smile trying to get him to not worry as much. Even when he followed her direction his face was saying otherwise.

He laid down undressed, he had his underwear on, and she exclaimed "oh no take everything off!" he obeyed in his quietness and laid on his front to the bed. She put drops of oil on his body randomly, his whole body was shivering from the coldness of the oil. Slowly massaged his whole back from his neck down to the toes, his blood was boiling up and finally even his mind could relax, and he drifted into peace and calmness.

In his relaxed state she spoons and cuddles him, her touch is a gentle balm, soothing his agitated spirit. She wraps him in her embrace and care, a sense of profound safety washed over him. She was so in his skin that her steady heartbeat sounded like a rhythmic lullaby, lulling his racing mind into tranquillity. He fell asleep like a baby and even when he woke up in the middle of the night, he just looked at her sleepy head besides him and he knew not to drift in worries. Her unwavering presence is a beacon of calmness guiding him back to the peaceful shores of his soul.

Ultimately all good things must come to an end. Like the saying "regression to the mean" which means no matter how good or terrible things can get they will always even out. Even their amazing night had to come to an end when alarms started beeping and they had classes to go to.

They started off their day on a high note even when Matthew pretended to be going to class which he did not. He dedicated his day to reading the book she had gifted him (The Alchemist).

At the Nkosi resident the silence was presiding over everything, even birds had an audience for their melodies. Since Mrs Nkosi came back, she has not uttered a single word to her husband, even himself he had his lips glued up with regret and shame. Mrs Nkosi knew her suspicion of being framed by her very own husband were real. Her husband had a hand in Advocate Mahlangu's murder, what she could not grasp was his cunning to make it look like it was her. Her suspension pending trial was hanging on her shoulders pulling her down the pits of anxiety and she had no pillar to hold on to.

Matthew was deeply focus on his reading journey, getting the wisdom and motivation to pursue his dreams. As he kept on reading, his visions and aspirations were becoming clearer and clearer with each paragraph he swallowed.

He reads out loud and repeat the phrase "remember that wherever your heart is, there you will find your treasure" He instilled the thought until he believed it. He knew exactly where his heart was. His heart started racing for adventure he took his new camera drove downtown reaching for his heart, and he found a perfect natural spot to take his portraits.

Mrs Nkosi was deep in her thoughts trying to visualize how she could counterattack the mountain that stood in the way of her career and reputation. She was done playing the victim and ready to plan for action to get herself back. Mr Nkosi was sitting across the room glimpsing at her and listening to her making phone calls to get favours from her connections and to prepare well for her trial. Mr Nkosi was even exhausted of trying to make small talks with her and not getting any reply, not even an energy of recognition.

Matthew was having a time of his life with the camera, without a care in the world. His passion took over his soul and body he spent hours taking snaps, from landscapes to flowers and roadways on an empty stomach and exhausted body, he could feel none of it. All the noises in the universe were mute to him and the only sound he could hear was the sharp percussive sound of the camera as he click on it to take his portraits. The movement of his fingers as he click to the perfection of his sight was so smooth and admirable you would swear the camera was invented for him.

Weeks passed by and Mr Nkosi had not heard a single word out of Mrs Nkosi's mouth directed at him since her arrest. The Nkosi mansion was quiet and cold, her heart was even colder, she never expected her husband to throw her under the bus to save his own skin. The hole he pieced in her heart left her hollow and dark she almost lost her sanity. The thought of fighting him was way behind her mind she needed only to get her ducks in a row to get herself out of the dungeon he put her in. Her feelings were so numb she could not even share a bed with him, they were living on separate wings of the mansion.

Weeks passed by Matthew was either taking pictures or reading (The Alchemist) he had no care in the world he did not even notice Sandra's absence and the lost bond between the two, he had found new love. He did not even realise the mid-year examinations were around the corner until he received an email stating he does not qualify to write the exams due to his unattendance of classes and the class tests he had missed. Even when he knew the content being taught, he did not realize skipping classes would have consequences. He knew he could pass the first-year examinations on a whim, yet he could not be allowed to write.

Mrs Nkosi was furious to receive statements of payment that depicted Matthew could not write his mid-year examinations. She had troubles of her own and Matthew was weighing more down her shoulders. She could not begin to fathom his inconsideration or what could have went wrong with him. She knew him to be a genius who could have passed the class tests with minimum effort. She called him right away; they exchanged unpleasant words, and he finally found his voice and told her he want to pursue photography, and he has never been interested in computer science. He ripped her heart out when he told her of how she messed up his childhood for him and that she cannot ruin his future as well.

Matthew has never felt so relieved. After the conversation he had with his mother telling her off and how he want to follow his passion of photography he felt on top of the world, except reality kicked him down. He received a second email that explained he could not continue with the institution for the rest of the year, since he could not write examinations for first semester modules, he had no business taking second semester modules because the first semester modules were a pre-requisite for second semester modules. As he was devasted and his head spinning he was served with a notice to evacuate the house before the end of the week.

Mrs Nkosi was prepared and ready for her trial. The reporters and social media were down her throat, and she was ready to conquer the world. She has never been this confident and she rightfully portrayed the phrase "you cannot keep a good man down". Nothing was going to tilt her head down except her own son who had only a few days to return from the state as a drop out. For once in her life, she did not care about people's opinions, and she sent Matthew two tickets one for his flight and the other to ship his car and luggage.

Matthew was yet faced with a difficult obstacle; his dream anc passion had found root in the United State of America, and he had no root for himself to stay in the state. The tickets from his mother came with the conditions that he must finish the year interning at her law firm in the ICT department until he can get another acceptance for the following year. Matthew was not having it, unfortunately he did not have a choice, he had no place to stay, no means of living and ultimately, he did not have a studio nor a platform to sell his pictures. His dream was only a fairy tale. To top it up he was still in self-doubt about the value of his pictures.

The courtroom went quiet as a grave when Mrs Nkosi entered for her first day of the trial. She was so confident; she was even mistaken for a psychopath murderer. Besides her was a team of lawyers from her firm who had serious faces to show how serious there were about the fight they were going to put up. She pleaded not guilty and the whole court exclaimed.

Matthew suddenly remembered he had a girlfriend, and he went to her place on his way out to the harbour to drop his car and head to the airport to catch his flight back home. Sandra was not pleased with him and his disappearing act on her, but she could not care less she was busy preparing for her first semester examinations. She despised him for skipping classes and test while she was under the impression that he was going.

Yet she felt guilty that this was her doing. "Well, you have a safe journey and do not be a stranger" she said to him, she could not even look into his eyes, hers were filled with anger, sadness, and disappointment. He drove off and she stood there until she could not see the car no more. She sent him a text right away that reads "never give up on your dreams, it is all you have that you own."

Mrs Nkosi's lawyers were able to depict without a reasonable doubt her whereabout on the night Advocate Mahlangu was murdered, she had received a call while in her sleep from her sister and she was on the call exactly around the time Advocate Mahlangu was murdered. They pointed the characteristics of the person wearing her dress in the CCTV footage as a male character and the court had no more arguments. It was ruled that she was framed. She was finally free she has never been so ecstatic, and the case had given her more publicity, that the public demanded her immediate reinstatement as the magistrate.

Matthew had decide to not give up on his dreams and he knew if he returned back home, they were as good as buried. He decided to take root where his dreams found theirs, even when he had no roof over his head, he had a car to live in and a little allowance he had left on his account. He decided to stay in the state, in his car with no plan to realize his dreams, only the faith and the will spirit. His computer programming skills came in handy when reality hit him that he was in a foreign country with no one to look after him but himself. He opened up a website and started publishing his portraits.

As much as he tried to keep up hope, when hope dwindles, it can be difficult to maintain motivation and enthusiasm. His dream was becoming distant and unattainable or so it seemed. He lost hope and just by taking sight of him I could tell he had lost direction; he was feeling stranded in his own maze.

Mrs Nkosi came back home a legend after her trial, and she was so proud she pulled herself out of the mud without dirtying anyone, even when she knew the person who framed her was none other than her own spouse. The victory was Her's, and she knew she could not lay with a betrayer anymore. She entered the mansion tipsy with a white envelop in her hand. She found Mr Nkosi sipping his whiskey and she dropped the envelope on his lap. He immediately opened it, and it was titled "Divorce Agreement." She was not having anyone mess with her anymore that even when she noticed Matthew did not board his flight, she cut him off financially.

It has been weeks Matthew staring at his screen with not a single offer made for his portraits. As much his portraits were alluring, he was a nobody, and no one knew of his website. He was on his last penny when he started to regret his choice of not going home. His stomach was growling in hunger that he started giving dustbins side-eyes whenever he would come across one. He had never missed the Nkosi mansion like that, except he refused to break and go crawling home.

Well, the way I see it I would say his state of finances also played a role, even if he wanted to go home how would he? But aside that he persisted even when the fire in his heart was becoming ashes with each day that passed, and he lost skin with each growl in his stomach. His hope, inspiration and enthusiasm starved to an almost death, his health and wellbeing was to follow until he reached out for help.

Sandra was surprised to receive a call from Matthew, it had been weeks since he left without even contact of his arrival at home. She picked up and he spoke "can you please meet me at the campus gates" she did not know whether to go or refuse him, but her heart yearned to see him.

The smile on Mrs Nkosi's face when she saw the various reactions of Mr Nkosi to the divorce settlement demands was priceless. He was a big-shot politician, but he knew not to mess with her on the legal front. Coupled with his guilty conscience he did not put much of a fight, he slid the papers back to the envelope quietly and went to his home office. His face was so frowned he gave her a side eye like he would just grab her with his eyes and swallow her. Her heart glowed like an emergency light out of her chest to the satisfaction of seeing his turmoil.

Sandra finally went to the campus gate to meet with Matthew, his eyes came to life when he saw her. Her skin was so fine, her eyes blossoming, she walked like she was not touching the ground, he lost his mind to the sight of her. She had played it in her mind and set out harsh words she was going to shoot him with, unfortunately her heart won over her mind, and she threw herself at him soon as he opened his arms for her. Through their hug she could tell he was not the same Matthew she knew, looking closely at him, his skin was crusty, in his dirty clothes and his eyes were evident he had not slept for weeks. Her heart bled and her tears failed her, he also broke down to the sight of her tears.

Mrs Nkosi finally breathed watching Mr Nkosi drive away, she was peeking at him from the balcony. She felt so much lighter knowing he was not coming back. He had signed off the Divorce Agreement that clearly stated he was to leave with only his clothes, one car and only ten thousand rand to his name. she was to keep everything else, from the mansion, their investments together and the name they built for themselves. She felt so relieved to not have to sleep with one eye open in her own sanctuary.

Matthew came crawling to his heart's sanctuary and everything got better, he felt renewed. He explained to her why he never went home and how determined he is to following his aspirations. Like she always know what he need when he does not, she advised him to not only rely on his website that is known only to him, but to enhance his social media presence from twitter, Facebook and Instagram that is where he can share his website and he should not be afraid of putting his best work out for free, "you can only get much better when you compete to better himself" she said to him and he knew she made a lot of sense.

"Wait here I am coming" she said, and he watched her walk away admiring her body as he moves. She was exactly his dream girl; her personality and compassion were just extras. Just when he thought she was taking forever he saw her approaching, changed and she was wearing a big red coat, winter was approaching, and the evenings had started getting colder. She pass by him as he was busy drooling over her and went straight to the passenger seat. He took a moment outside the car trying to pull himself together, so he does not drool much, but it did not help.

Soon as he entered the car, with his eyes fixed on her, she commanded "drive" he answered, "well you do realize I live in this car, right? where are we going?" "Do you trust me?" she spoke confidently he could not deny, but she noticed him looking at his gas gauge "first we stop by the filling station, and I will direct you exactly where we are going" she spoke and settled in her seat. Without further questions he decided to trust her, and he stopped at the nearest petrol station. She filled up his car and coming back from the store she came with two full plastic bags which she dumbed at the trunk of his car where his whole life was tucked in.

They drove for two straight hours as per her direction and they ended up in the middle of nowhere at a cabin near a dark lake. Soon as the engine went off and the car lights died, it was the darkest they have ever seen, the quietest they have ever experienced. They approached the cabin with Sandra leading the way. She took out keys in her left pocket of the coat, she unlocked and went straight for the lights and the cabin lived. Before he could say anything all the questions were right on his face and she answered "well this is my uncle's cabin, he is in China at the moment, I am responsible for checking it every now and then, and now you are going to stay here until you find your feet" she said handing the keys to him.

He was so overwhelmed he just grabbed and squeezed her into his arms. He was filled with so much gratitude he did not have words for it. He kept on saying "thank so much" squeezing and looking at her, he could not believe it. "won't you get into trouble for this?" he asked her out of concern, and she replied "do not worry about me, anyone who want to come here will contact me first that is the only key, and my uncle entrusted it with me" she answered and assure him.

They went to the car to fetch his stuff and the groceries she bought him; within a few moments they were settled in. It is always the coldest around the lake. Matthew went to get firewood behind the cabin as she directed him, and they put on a fire while she prepared supper and he packed his stuff away and helped to clear the dust in the shelves and cupboards. Within a considerable amount of time, they were both done and ready to eat. He was surprised to come and find his plate filled up all around, just as he stammered in disbelief she laughed and commented "well, look at yourself, you need to eat and get back to the Matt I know" he laughed sat down and they ate.

Sandra finished first and as he finished up his plate, she was standing by the kitchen door behind him and she said "well come on now, let mommy wash you up, am sure you haven't had a good bath in ages" indeed his skin was ev dent enough that he had not bathed well for quite some time, if he has bathed at all. He was so full he did not have any energy to argue with her he just put his dish by the sink and followed her to the bathroom.

Matthew's solitude has messed up his mind, he became so stupor he did not even know how to act around her. His thoughts were still wild trying to process all she has done for him and how she always got his back. He stared on the bathroom mirror with his eyes blurred by the tears he was fighting so hard to hold back. She hugged him from behind and directed him to undress, he did and went straight to the bathtub. The water was warmer he could not sit straight.

She undressed after him and threw herself in the bathtub as well. The scent around the room was so flowery and therapeutic. She started washing him from his arms and chest and he just stood there gawking at her sexy body when she moved around to handle all parts of his body. The bulb in his brains finally caught power and lit up, he also grabbed a towel and started washing her instead of looking at her body like a mad man.

Unfortunately, the water could only become colder with each second that passed, as much as they enjoyed washing each other and catching up naked they started shivering from cold. They jumped out of the water; they stood side by side applying lotion on their bodies. She finished first as he had only put lotion in his hands and stared at her from the mirror as she was applying her own. She left the bathroom, and he regained his senses, he started to feel how cold it was, he finished up and found her sitting by the couch next to the fireplace covered in a blanked over his shirt she was wearing.

He went and sat next to her and she overlayed the blanked on his lap and he covered himself with it. "Are you okay" she asked him when she felt his body vibrating as he shivers from cold. "Yes, am good" he replied. He continued to shiver, and she moved closer, hugged him, and laid her head on his chest. He reached out his hand to hold her, he grabbed her waist with one hand as she was playing with and warming up the other. He slowly moved his hand down the waist to her ass where he skipped a breath when he touched and realised, she went commando.

He then started brushing her ass from under the blanket he licked his lips while doing it, they were getting drier with each touch. His eyes could not be kept open, the more and harder he rubbed her, the more his senses became dull to everything else but the sensation of her skin. She increased the grip on his other hand just as she squeezed her legs together, and the rate of her breath increased. The next thing he knew his hand was in humid places and came out wet. She could not take the pressure no more, she abruptly got up and sat on top of him with her knees on either side of his thighs, she kissed him so fast and violently while both her hands were reaching inside his trouser.

Soon as she grabbed his penis, she could not wait to take his pants off, she slid it through her virginal fluids right inside of her, she yelled in pleasure as it filled her up and he grabbed her ass cheeks so hard you would swear he was about to make them vanish into his palms. She continued to moan as they were sweating all over each other and Matthew's hands would move from her ass to her boobs and she kept of riding him like a Texan cowboy.

They were so tired no one was up to getting up from the couch even when they could feel it was not comfortable for the both of them to lay there together. In a moment they finally got up and headed to the bedroom. They threw themselves on bed and they cuddled each other to sleep. That was the best and comfortable Matthew had slept in weeks and he just dozed off like a baby. Sandra herself had not slept much better than sleeping while watching Matthew's dead asleep face.

Hope dawns with every day, Sandra was already up by 6h00am in the morning. So much as she enjoyed the sight of Matthew's sleepy head, she had to wake him up so he can take her back to campus. After a while of struggling to get him fully awake she finally managed, and he woke up to the road. In an hour and a half, he dropped her at the campus gate, and she rushed off to prepare for her class.

Matthew waited around for a moment, and it hit him hard watching student his age moving around campus with smile and hunger on their faces to get their diplomas and he was only a few months drop out, smart as he was. He watched with admiration and envy until he got inspired to go and work on his dream. On his way back to the cabin he visited several studios for inspiration and to make connections with people in the industry. He spend his day moving around town from studio to studio grabbing advice and contacts.

It has been two weeks now Matthew wakes up each day going to town attending art seminars, meeting legends in the industry, collecting contacts and preaching about his website. It has all been going well, he was motivated than ever until one morning when he started his car and realize he was empty on gas. He sat in the car for quite a while demoralized, he did not have a cent on him, and he did not want to bother Sandra who has already given a handful. He had no one else and he just sat there watching his motivation and energy crushing to pieces.

He spent the entire day wallowing sitting by the lake side. He looked back at how his life was going so well; he had moved from the villages to the state, to one of the best universities money can buy, he found the girl of his dreams and he had friends. He kept on trying to figure out what went wrong, with no answers to any of his questions. "Why did I not just finish the damn degree, get a good job and live happily ever after?" he spoke out loud asking himself. Sandra was worried he has not heard from him that day that he was in town, she got worried, and she sent him a text that reads:

"Never crumble at the sight of a hill, that is a chance to create your imagined path. If and when you come across a hill, I trust you to carve it out and create a slide for your smooth sail."

The text came together with several other beeps, he got intrigued to check his phone. Right after reading her text just as he was grasping hope and realizing what a smart woman he have. He checked the other notification to realize one of his portraits had got over a dozen of orders paid in full. He jumped with joy he immediately called Sandra "Sanz you will not believe this" he exclaimed excited, and she was curious to hear it "I just received fully paid orders of one of the sunset pictures I took on our first date" he spoke in a rush she did not hear much but she could tell it was good news.

This was not an order to set him up, but it was enough to ignite his passion and the limping dream inside of him. He kept pacing up and down in delight, it was a miracle to see that this passion of his can actually bring money in. He got a lifeline exactly when he needed one. To you fellow dreamer out there never give up, let every move you make set you up for success and draw you closer and closer to your promised land. No matter how silly or irrelevant you dream seem, if you build it high enough you can make wealth out of it.

Matthew had thought, him going to town everyday attending seminars, visiting studios, art galleries and collecting contacts were all a waste of time and gas when he was not getting any positive feedback. What he did not realize was that each and everything has its waiting season. The season to grind, the season to find your path, the season to prepare for what is to come and the season to harvest.

Everything worth having has a high price to pay. Even when he felt defeated and thinking of going home to fulfil his parent's dream he never gave up, he kept on grinding, and he had his community who knew how to lift him up when he needed a stone to step on. He had a beautiful woman by his side who supported him through and through.

Sandra was the best part of Matthew, and he knew it. Weeks passed by and he kept on receiving orders and invites. His name was being spoken in big rooms; he was getting to be a well-known upcoming photographer with an eye for landscape photography. With all the attention he has been getting he decided to capitalize on it and open his own studio. "I already found a space, am just left with your blessings and your company when I go check it out" he talked smiling onto Sandra's face, they were in his car just outside the campus gate when he visited her to tell her the good news and ask for her blessings.

"I am flattered, and I will be your company, but did you manage to get hold of your mother?" she asked him with a serious face. "It has been a week now trying to get hold of her, but she is not taking my calls, and she seems busy, her face has been flying all over the papers back home" he tried to explain to her, and she was not convinced. "I am so happy for you my love, and you have all my blessings, but you also need your parents blessings" he frowned on her and he said "well my dad is cool, and he will be coming for the opening, once we can get the place and set the date" he answered her warming up on her so she could let the issue slide away and understand the urgency of getting a space.

Scene 08

"You don't have to be great to start, but you have to start to be great"-Zig Ziglar

Despite the safety, the satisfaction and self-fulfilment Miss Nkcsi was basking in for the past few weeks, the mansion was starting to feel lonely and empty. She was happy every morning heading to the job of her dreams, yet she was sad every evening coming back to an empty and cold mansion. She even got to a point of desperation, she started going to male strip clubs where she found herself a young man who was willing to satisfy her sexual needs and she would take care of him financially.

It was early hours of the evening, Miss Nkosi was up her balcony, waiting for her sex partner when she realised that as much as she was getting a lot of sexual attention, she needed a companion who is not just for sex. She looked at how her life had turned out, how her dream family had fallen apart, she shed a tear. She took her phone looked up Matthew to realize she had not unblocked him since she did the last time she talked to him, and he would not agree with her conditions for coming back home.

She unblocked him right away and hit him up. "Ma! is that you?" Matthew was delighted to receive his mother's call. She did not know what to say she continued in silence, and he said to her "I have been trying to get hold of you this past week, I have good news". She finally spoke and asked, "what good news" he answered her "as we are speaking, I am viewing what the interior designer has done to my studio, it is so stunning Ma!" he spoke out of excitement. It was a perfect moment for him talking to his mother and watching his girlfriend move around the place checking it out in admiration.

He continued catching up with his mother, he was filled with outmost joy, and she felt a sense family and contentment. Although she did not approve of his choice of career, she was finally proud of him and how he spoke like a boss. "Yes, the 1st of august" he emphasized to her after she asked to confirm the date of his studio launch. Having talked to her son helped her perspective, right after the call she called her sex partner and told him to not come anymore, she will no longer be needing his services. She realized what a grown-up son she got, and her sex partner was just two years older than her son.

Day before the launch Mr and Miss Nkosi were in the same plane headed to the states in California for their son's studio launch and neither of them knew they boarded the same flight. With luck they both managed to arrive without noticing each other. Mr Nkosi went to fetch his hired car, so did she and when they both arrived at the hotel reception an unfortunate miracle happened when the receptionist called out "Nkosi" and they both stepped forward.

They were estranged to each other they had not seen each other since the day they finalised their divorce, except in the media. "Well, is it a Mr or a Miss?" with emphasis on Miss, Mr Nkosi asked the receptionist without taking his eyes off Miss Nkosi. "Uhm, there is only Nkosi, it does not say whether it is a Mr or a Miss" she spoke out loud with her voice breaking out of the confusion and the Mistake she made of taking The Nkosi bookings as one instead of making separate reservation.

They spent hours at the reception trying to get the mix-up rectified with no luck. The hotel was booked out and they had no choice but to share the suit. Miss Nkosi was not having it; she was not about to share a room with the man who sold her out and threw her to the wolves. They bickered for hours until Mr Nkosi gave up the room to Miss Nkosi. He drove around town looking for motels, finally he found one, it was not decent as the hotel, but he just needed a place to lay his head down after the day he just had and being jet legged.

It was a cold night in the state for the Nkosi family, Mr Nkosi could not get his mind off Miss Nkosi since he laid his eyes on her. Miss Nkosi could not get his mind off Mr Nkosi since she laid her eyes on him, even when her heart missed him, she could not get over his betrayal and she slept with a heavy heart, her mind battled her heart. Matthew was having a night of his life with Sandra, but he could not shake off the anxiety of meeting his parents, especially with the divorce between them.

The day of the launch, everything was set and ready except the man of the moment. Luckily, he woke up next to the goddess of his dreams. He was so excited, and his nerves were getting the best of him. "Well, you kept tossing and turning last night, are you okay?" those were Sandra's first words soon as she cracked open her eyes. "Look everything you have been through, all those downs and the nights you slept in a car, they were all leading up to this evening" she continued to speak staring at the anxiety and fear in his eyes.

He listened to her, and he knew she was right but none of what she said could mute the voices in his head. She took a leap of faith when she jumped off her sleeping position and sat on his lap from where he was sitting beside her on the bed, she put both her palms behind his heard brushing him and she said "hey look at me" it worked like magic, and everything went all quiet. He finally listened she said "this is your day to be the man you were always meant to be, from today onward you get to live in the realm of your dreams and most importantly go out there and show those who are still dreaming that it is possible" she spoke so slowly he grasped each and every single word as it came out of her mouth.

She knew he heard her when she felt his manhood rising between her thighs and his eyes buried in her cleavage. The event was not until 15h00 that evening, and they had plenty of time to fool around until then. When she felt his penis rising below her thighs, she did not hesitate widening them up giving it proper space. She whispered into his ears as she positioned herself well for better penetration position "I love you so much" before he could utter any word, he lost his breath to the sensational feeling he experienced when his penis grew and slid in her vagina, she rolled her eyes uttering sweet nothings with her mute mouth wide open.

"Tell me a story" she whispered again while riding on top of him so slowly and passionately he could not get in alignment with the pace of her breathing. Before he knew it, he caught up to her rhythm and he finally spoke "well there was once a young man who flew across the world to fulfil a dream, except it was not his dream, on his journey he found a beautiful, amazing woman and he knew from the first glance she was his rib, ...ohhh sh*t" he could not finish his story his feelings were sky up and she dared him to continue, as she continued riding and increasing speed with every heavy breath he took "what he never appreciated was the fact that he had a free ride to his dream city with a spear in his right hand to carve out his dream in a city where it was all possible" just as she was about to climax she yelled "did he succeeeeeeeeeed" "oh yes he did, yes he did, yes he did" he also screamed it out "yes he did" a couple of times just as he was ejaculating inside of her.

After the moment they just had he was feeling more ready and determined to conquer the day. His inbox was flooding with the RSVP's from industry friends and mentors, he felt even more content to the knowledge that his parents are also in the city to witness his achievements. His heart has never been in the right place right until this moment when he looked at everything around him and it was all about him. He was doing what he love, what he enjoys, and he had the privilege of doing it with the woman of his dreams.

"In whatever you do, never let your dreams die off while you live on, make it your purpose to fulfil them in your lifetime."

Matthew looked the dream in the eye, and he has never been prouder of himself. He looked in the mirror he saw a man for the first time ever. He did not need assurances and directions from his parents, he was on his own self-made path. He was content in his journey, he felt goosebumps every time he held a camera, and all the times he went on adventures to take pictures of beautiful and unique lancscapes.

He could not believe his eyes after waiting hours for Sandra to finish up. She entered the room, like a storm she was, she blew everything in the room even he was blown away to the view he saw as she stepped in. Each step she took he anticipated, until she could come closer to him, and he finally caught his breath the moment he rested his arms on her waist. "You look so stunning" he said. Those were not the words he wanted to utter, even he did not know the words, but she saw them all over his face.

Like a power couple they went to the car holding hands, he could not let go of her. They arrived early at the venue to ensure everything was to their standard and satisfaction, it was. His parents arrived next, and the four went to what was to be his office. Over the wall was a big depiction of a landscape he took from home. Mr and Miss Nkosi both realized he has always been good at photography right under their noses. Even with their faces frowned at each other, it did not stop them from appreciating their son's art and talent.

The atmosphere and the energy in the room was just as expected it would be. "Mom, dad this is Sandra she is my girlfriend, and she is the one who helped me realise all of these" he said demonstrating with his hands, pointing all around the office. "Hello, my girl" Mr Nkosi broke the ice right after Matthew finished the introductions between Sandra, his mother, and his father. Miss Nkosi kept quiet and honestly that was the best she could do, considering her mood being in the same room as Mr Nkosi and how last time she had a chat with Matthew's girlfriend Elsa, Matthew never heard from her ever since.

Sandra was smart enough to read the room, and she knew she was misplaced. "Well, I will leave you to it" she said after greeting both Mr and Miss Nkosi. She stepped outside before neither could respond to her. It was written all over Matthew's face that he was not going to let her leave him with his parents by himself. Yet she left, he had to face his parents alone. "Please can you two get along just this evening, for me, please!" he finally pleaded to both of them after long hours of catching up and absorbing the tension between the two. He could tell there was a bigger issue but none of them could tell him, the real reason of their divorce.

Minutes dropped down like drops of water on a waterfall. With each minute down the river pushing time closer to the start of the event. Guests started arriving gradually, Matthew got more anxious with every peek he took from the back as he saw the audience increasing. Mr and Miss Nkosi went to blend in with the crowd. They sat across each other in the hall, one on either side on the room, yet they could not keep their eyes off each other.

A suffocating emptiness gnawed at their chests, as they watched couples around the room and all they could grasp was a constant reminder of love lost and dreams shattered for their perfect family. The energy and love that was flying in the room was just so overwhelming, that

Matthew made over a Million rands before he could even introduce himself and declare the studio officially opened nor before they could start with the auctions.

Finally, everyone was called to attention after a moment of socializing and getting comfortable with snacks and glasses of champagnes flying around the room. Matthew was overwhelmed with feelings of anxiety and appreciation at once. He had never before spoken in front of such a huge crowd, and yet despite his fear of public speaking that room was a depiction of his vision and dream. "Leave out reality and step into the dream" Sandra spoke while fixing his coat when she could feel his trembling and his heart beating faster.

The room went quiet as empty, when he was announced to the stage to give his speech. He stepped in the room, and he could hear echoes of his footsteps, his heart pounding the loudest. He stood at the podium, and he felt every eye in the room gawking at him, each ear itching waiting to be relieved by the melody of his voice. His hands started shaking, and his whole-body trembling, he looked like he was about to faint. For a moment everyone was worried about him, and at last he stepped into the dream.

"Live the dream, to become the dream; the longer you live the dream the stronger the foundation you have, the greater the chance you stand of pushing the door until it opens. Keep pushing until you step into that dream."

He spoke so well; he owned the room. Everyone's faces lit with hope, desire, and drive to follow their dreams to the fullest, when he shared the story of his journey. His story inspired the young and the old. He stepped into his dreams and gave others courage to sleep more and dream more. Matthew went on about his speech he even deviated from what he had written, he spoke from the heart. He grabbed the room's attention, had everyone wrapped around his fingers when he said:

"Born into riches, I declared myself poor for the one's I was born into were not mine. To everyone who still have a dream inside of them, never be afraid of the grind, never be afraid of being different and never accept failure if you can still try again."

Often times we tend to get comfortable around the materialistic things around us and fail to pursue our own hearts. We sit comfortably on luxurious couches and forget to build our own. We get comfortable in fame and names our parents built that we live in their shadows and dim our lights. Let the foundation you are born on, fuel you to be better, no matter how tiny or great it is.

He continued with his speech, and just as he was about to wrap up, his chest started ponding, his closing lines momentarily forgotten. The expectants faces in the crowd started to blur as his gaze landed on what he wanted to believe was a figment of Elsa. The lady was in disguise she had a hoodie over her head covering bits of her face moving at the back rows headed to the exit, soon as she realized him staring her way. His mind raced, trying to comprehend this unexpected twist of fate as he struggled to regain his composure and continue with his speech.

"Thank you" he spoke to the crowd cutting his speech so abruptly everyone was shocked. But the surrounding landscapes in the walls shined over his premature cut of speech. People continued to mingle and enjoy the overflowing of art and entertainment while he ran through the back door to try and catch the lady, he thought was Elsa. He ran like a headless chicken when he saw her moving so fast across the streets, as he ran trying to catch her and his breath, he caught his breath when he stopped after seeing her getting into a metered taxi.

He started to believe it was not who he thought she was when she stepped in the taxi, and he realized that the lady was pregnant, almost ready to give birth. He returned back to meet Sandra who was out following behind him in surprise to where he was headed to in such a rush. "Babe who was that?" she asked with a faint voice catching up her breath. "I have no idea, I thought she was someone, I guess not" he answered her with his eyes fixated to the direction the taxi took, much as he wanted to believe it was not Elsa, he strongly believed what he saw.

Well, if you could ask me, I would like to say I am the observer of all and I can confirm that Matthew's instinct was right. It was her, undeniably her. He surely saw his ex-girlfriend Elsa on the biggest day of his life, and she is indeed pregnant, for who it is not my question to answer.

To be continued!!!

Acknowledgments

A heartfelt thank you to all those who have supported me on this journey. Your encouragement and belief in this story have been invaluable. I'm profoundly grateful for your enthusiasm and patience.

I would also like to express my gratitude to the readers who have followed me on this adventure. Your feedback, comments, and reviews have been a constant source of inspiration.

A Note to Readers

This is just the beginning. The story will continue in the next book, [WITHIN THE DREAM]. Get ready for more twists, turns, and unforgettable adventures.

Thank you again for joining me on this journey. I cannot wait to share more with you in the future.

www.ingramcontent.com/pod-product-compliance
Lightning Source LLC
LaVergne TN
LVHW041216150826
845673LV00001B/427

* 9 7 8 1 0 3 7 0 1 2 0 9 9 *